The Memoirist

The Memoirist

Neil Williamson

NewCon Press
England

First published in the UK by NewCon Press
41 Wheatsheaf Road, Alconbury Weston, Cambs, PE28 4LF
March 2017

NCP 115 (limited edition hardback)
NCP 116 (softback)

10 9 8 7 6 5 4 3 2 1

ISBN:

978-1-910935-35-4 (hardback)
978-1-910935-36-1 (softback)

Cover art by Chris Moore
Cover layout by Andy Bigwood

Minor editorial meddling by Ian Whates
Book layout by Storm Constantine

One

"*Et bien*, have you done your homework, Miss Fitzgerald?"

The question from the kitchen caught me off guard. I was finding the apartment a minefield of distractions: the threadbare damask couch rough under my fingers, the constellation of unswept detritus on the parquet, the little Moroccan table that held a blown glass ashtray and a pair of Intaface glasses, deactivated and by the looks of them hardly used. My client wasn't a fan of technology; hence the reason I'd gone in person to Paris instead of conducting the interview by face in a professional manner.

A rustle tugged my attention towards the house plants in artisanal pots that lined the window sill, a breeze-shivered profusion of greenery tumbling from in front of the louvres along with muted Parisian street sounds. The room was cool and crepuscular, and beneath the smell of old cigarettes and fresh coffee there was also a musty, avian odour.

The first thing that my attention had settled on when I'd entered was the birdcage. It was squeezed into shelves thick with knickknacks, books and faded magazines, door open, perch swinging empty. The occupant had waited until my hostess had gone to prepare refreshments before descending on me from the curtain rail in a fluster of wings and glossy black. Golden-browed and preening on a chair back, that creature more than anything else in the room was distracting me. Sitting there in my best suit, I felt scrutinised, under suspicion, like a home visit banker with bad news.

Had I done my homework? "Yes, of course." I smiled professionally, but already had misgivings as to how our meeting was going to play out.

The interview is mostly for gloss. Clients think it's their stage from which to deliver the definitive story of their lives. Most actually believe that you distil their memoir directly from their rambling armchair reminiscences. No matter that most of the information is already freely available and that the good memoirist has already assembled the facts before the interview takes place. Which isn't to say that the chat isn't important. It's when you get a feel for the subject's voice, and when you find out how they want to spin the story of their life; what they want featured front and centre, and what they want discreetly glossed over. But as for the meat of the story? By that point it's in the can.

"You were born Elodie Barthelme, in Avignon, France, seventeenth August, nineteen ninety." As I spoke, I blinked open my face, kicked off the session recorder and slid the transparency of the window containing the biography to twelve percent. "You ran away to Paris aged fourteen, and then to London at seventeen. Formed electro-rock outfit The HitMEBritneys with John Eagles, who later became your first husband –"

"Blah, blah, etcetera, etcetera. But do you believe all that?" My client reappeared, perching on the edge of the armchair and crossing her legs. The black polish on the toes peeking from the cuffs of her combats was chipped, and when she leaned forward it was evident that she was wearing no underwear beneath her chemise. I caught myself staring. So did she. Yet again I wished we were doing face to face.

"Sorry?"

"That stuff from the wikis. Do you believe it?" Her accent came and went, swinging between precise French and Estuary English.

"I always draw my research from a number of sources." I tried not to sound peevish.

"From other wikis?" Her smirk was glossy.

I swallowed a retort, hearing Pawel's chide: *She's right, Fizz. Wikis stopped being the bastions of independence and self-regulation way back when governments started building whole departments to monitor and edit them.*

Pawel had never got what I did: my discreetly sculpted memoirs. *Comfortable death-bed lies,* he called them. He claimed to believe in truth. Real, *true* truth. But the subjects of memoirs aren't interested in truth. What they want is hagiography and valediction. Usually that can be achieved by drawing selectively from what is in the public domain. And when it can't...there are ways to play it. There's always scope for a shocking revelation.

"I cross-reference with a *number* of sources," I said. "Is any of what I've said inaccurate?"

The black bird had found a new perch atop the bookcase and chose that moment to let out a startling whistle. Elodie cracked a smile. "It's close enough." She glanced up. "Isn't that so, Lysander?"

The bird shuffled, hopped to a stack of National Geographics. Then it opened its yellow bill. "Close enough," it croaked.

Curiosity winning out, I winked up a window in my face, entering: *bird, pet, mimic human speech.*

"How do you take your coffee?"

I didn't answer immediately because a flag was flashing. A problem with the recorder. Aside from a range of potentially dire legalities, the last thing I needed was another messy job. Any number of prospective clients could be watching me work before they decided to initiate contact... or go elsewhere. I could feel my proticks tumbling.

"White please." I detested coffee. "No sugar."

The recorder hadn't started. I breathed out in relief.

Audiovisual recording failure. WatchNet has no source at your location.

Stupidly, I scanned the room again and this time, among the cosy and the kitsch, I spotted what I'd missed. There was sparkwire dangling from the light fitting, a fringe of delicate mesh visible around the window frame.

"You've no bees in here," I said as Elodie Eagles returned with a pot and tiny cups. The pungent stain of the coffee spread around the room.

"Well spotted." She tossed aside the face set to make room on the table. "No milk, you'll have to have it black, I'm afraid."

Then why did you ask me how I liked it? I was too well trained to say that aloud to her retreating back, but if anyone had been watching they'd have been able to read it in my expression. I calmed myself and attempted to concentrate on the job in hand.

"HitMEBritneys had modest success in the UK and Europe," I said brightly, "but failed to catch on in the US, which was still the prime market for global music sales before China and Brazil rose to dominance."

"We didn't do it for global sales." Elodie returned again with an oval plate patterned with flowers, pastel petals interlocking. It was loaded with long, delicate biscuits. "*Longue-du-chat,*" she said. "Just out of the oven."

"No? That must have been unique for the noughties." She stared at me until I took a biscuit, tasted it. It was warm and sweet and buttery. I savoured it while she poured.

She sat back in the armchair, took a sip. "We did it to see what would happen." There was a glint in her eyes then, and I knew why she had invited me here to France instead of meeting over the face. All this distraction. She was pressing my buttons, to see how I would react.

Even though no one was watching, I sat up straight, brushed crumbs from my skirt. "And is that why you decided to have a memoir written too? To see what will happen?"

Right then Elodie Eagles paled, shrank in her chair and for the first time looked like a sixty-seven year old woman. Or, rather, that was how it seemed. All that really happened was that that the cocksure challenge that she had been famous for all her life faded from her eyes and, with it, the glamour that she was still the feisty teenager who had whipped audiences into a frenzy in the noughties, who had started riots, been arrested in more than one country on charges ranging from affray to obscenity. Neither was she the glamorous queen bitch, Marietta, who for thirteen seasons had terrorized the other characters in the hugely popular Euro-soap, *The Days*.

No, she was just another ageing semi-celebrity realizing how little time there was left, and trying to find a way to sum it up. To cash in, or perhaps set up one final grapple with fame following a tawdrily stage-managed exposé. I saw the pursed skin around that painted mouth, the white down on her lip, the clawing of age around her eyes. There were blue smudges of tattoos beneath her shirt. I'd seen the footage of how she used to self-ink them during her gigs. Once they had been no-logo logos, anti-establishment trademarks. To me they looked like old bruises, as if life had handed her a beating.

I felt more certain of myself. I was supposed to be the expert after all. "Well?"

Elodie Eagles' smile was tired. "Perhaps, yes," she said. "Partly." She sighed then, covered her eyes with her hands before dragging her fingers down her cheeks. "But mainly, Miss Fitzgerald, because I want to remember."

"To remember?" That surprised me because my clients usually prove capable of remembering altogether far too much, most of which is irrelevant even as froth or colour.

She nodded stiffly. "I have a brain... *disease.*" Even that generic word was difficult for her. She practically had to spit it out. To me, though, it explained a lot. I'd had several clients who, at the time of requesting a memoir, had become ill. Often I tried to help them see the illness itself as part of their story, that audiences would react warmly to a tragic ending bravely borne. In Elodie's case I was thinking *Alzheimer's*, *Parkinson's*, perhaps the first pension payouts after a career of substance abuse. I could have asked but, now that we were speaking honestly, my instinct was to let her tell me in her own time.

"The moths have been at my memory," she said, "Particularly my younger days. There was a lot of shit, sure. Stupid naivety and crazy, kid fun... perhaps a little beyond fun. But there were days of truth. Nights that mattered." I heard a hitch in her breath, saw a shudder ripple her pale cheeks. "There was one night..."

"You ever heard of a mynah?" The aproned waiter slipped a condensation-misted *pression* in front of me and I felt myself relax. A gauze of face windows masked the basilica of Notre Dame which dazzled me after the cloister of Elodie Eagles' Left Bank apartment. I was going over the wikis again, the music press archives, the fan sites too, and attempting to get myself into her mind set with a media loop of her greatest hits. Right now she was squatting on stage, stippling the letters *NOSX* into her arm with a pin, her fingers dripping blood and ink, her face set in a determined scowl.

Elodie's early lyrics had struck out at just about every target available to her at the time: environmental concerns, world poverty, cosy crypto-fascism and the nascent surveillance society. In her first album, especially, the establishment got kicked repeatedly in the face. A thirty five minute, brutal *screw you* to the society of the day.

NOSX: No Secrets, was her jab at the laws promoting erosion of online privacy, introduced by the same government who had been caught in historical cover-ups of institutionalised child sex abuse by senior party figures. If the people couldn't have secrets, she had reasoned, then no one should. It had been an angry but futile protest that had caused a bit of fuss at the time but in the long run had barely even been noticed by Europe's lawmakers who had been trimming those rights ever since under an assortment of labels: anti-terrorism, personal security, open data, free market, even local authority cutbacks.

The corner of my vision displayed a meandering view of the corner of *Quai St Michel* as seen through WatchNet's ubiquitous bees. Not actual bees, of course; those tiny airborne cameras only resembled the insects that gave them their name in size and the sound their wings made as they drifted by. I hadn't realised how reassuring I found the whirr and stir of their gentle tour until my visit with Elodie. This was the world I knew, busy and accessible. And here was me in the café at the corner, still looking every inch the professional.

"You look like someone stuck a broom handle up your ass," had been Pawel's first comment when he called to find out how I got on. Now he chuckled. "Like a mynah bird, you mean? Vicious fuckers. My auntie had one."

"They mimic you," I said.

"Don't be fooled," Pawel replied, and at that moment a breeze tugged at the curtain behind him, blazing his face with contrast. "It's just sound repetition, not intelligence."

"Where are you?" The brief glimpse had showed me he wasn't at home. If it was warm enough for him to have a window open, he was a long way from Bergen, or wherever he claimed to be this week.

His answer was a minute shake of the head.

Warned off, I sighed, took a sip of my beer, and then went back to telling him what had happened. Since he expressed no surprise by the lack of bees at Elodie's place, I assumed he'd attempted to eavesdrop.

"You don't think that's weird?" When I first got to know Pawel I'd tried to do a little snooping, with zero success. Well, everyone does it. Of course, WatchNet allows intrusion locks on designated private spaces – bedrooms and bathrooms, usually –

but everyone at some time or another has attempted to piggyback a bee hoping for a few seconds of scandal before its little quantum mind adjudges the scene not for public consumption. It was amazing what you could see with a little perseverance. Pawel, though, was a freelance consultant for various governments, and subsequently had an insanely hardline approach to privacy. No one ever saw anything of him that he didn't want them to.

And yes, even though I talked to his smiling face most days, the question of whether those familiar features were *really him* sometimes kept me awake. I suspected that he had his own bees, linked seamlessly into the system, digitally processing in real time what they saw. But what's a face? I was comfortable enough with what we shared.

Now, he just laughed. "Do I think it's weird that someone mistrusts WatchNet's security to the extent that she fries any bees that wander within her walls? Sounds like healthy scepticism to me." Then he added in the same breezy tone: "It is Alzheimer's by the way."

"How do you know?" I snapped. To Pawel everything was a joke. He was a Stensen-Brand baby – poster boy for the special kind of narcissistic superiority complex that came from a life lived exclusively online. Most of the time I found his confidence sexy, this was one of the few exceptions. Something about Elodie Eagles' plight had snagged me emotionally.

"I did my homework." He still couldn't resist the mocking tone. As he spoke, a packet of files from a Paris medical centre appeared in my face.

I ignored them for now. "How long has she had it?"

"Not long." He shrugged. "But they've tried the usual things, the drugs, the ultrasound. Nothing's even slowing it down."

"Long enough to start losing the memories she cares about," I said. "And apparently ones there are no records for."

"Pah," Pawel scoffed. "There are always records."

I shook my head. "Not for this one. It was the band's final

gig. Up in Glasgow, a legendary night. When the authorities prevented them from playing some political benefit, apparently Elodie dropped the band and gathered the fans for a guerrilla solo gig."

The news reports I'd been able to find slanted the story in different ways. The generous ones said it was the natural end of a spent force, the rest cried *prima donna*. I'd already tried contacting the band members themselves. The drummer had died of an early heart attack, and John Eagles, who had spent much of his life defending his ex-wife, replied to my extensive and carefully worded request with two infuriating words: *Ask Elodie*.

"There's a lot of media coverage from the trouble that led up to it. But nothing from the gig itself."

"You're just not looking smart enough, Fizz."

My file on that night already contained links to old blog entries, an NME front page, news reports of the riot and subsequent court cases, caches of long defunct fan group message boards of the sort that had practically been medieval even in the 2020's when Elodie's following was at its peak. And Pawel was right, even in those pre-bees days, for a band as popular as HitMEBritneys it was highly unusual to find not even a handful of blurry gig snaps, a few minutes of shaky cell phone footage, *somewhere*. Of course, I'd done no more than shave the surface of the dead icebergs of discarded social media accounts, the publicly accessible stuff. Anything buried in the private areas, or ambiguously titled or mis-dated, would require skills. I shared the file with Pawel. "Consider that a challenge," I said.

"This is a favour, right?" He was already scrolling through the links. Today he was using glasses, like Elodie's, and the silvering around his eyes shivered as new windows popped open in the lenses.

"Same deal as always," I replied. "If you come up with something I can use."

"Uh, huh. And what will you be doing when I'm digging out your nuggets of gold?"

"Only assembling the entire rest of her memoir."

The quizzical twist around his lips indicated that he thought that there wouldn't be a memoir without the information I'd tasked him to find. That wasn't true. Elodie Eagles had lived three times the life of most. There was plenty for me to sift through and order into narrative. But I had the same niggle as Pawel: that it wasn't just a cherished memory for her. Something important had happened that night in Glasgow.

I could not imagine what, of all the shows she had played in her life, was so singular that the loss of this one night from her memory caused her such distress. The local authority had used licensing legislation to block the band's original performance at an anti-capitalism rally. They didn't hear about the stealthily arranged solo spot until it was over, but there had been running battles throughout the city centre. It all painted a picture of an anti-establishment Boudica, an anarcho-warrior queen leading her tribe in angry rebellion. But was that really her crowning moment in her own mind? Was she such an egoist? I might have believed that before meeting her, but now it didn't feel quite right.

I drained my glass, flicking through the documents and watching the flow of Parisian life. Tourists strolling, diners perusing the café's menu, uniformed schoolchildren rising from the Metro like a flowering of forest bluebells. All of them covered, for their safety, their security, their peace of mind, close to all of the time by WatchNet's bees. And – this was the best bit – if anything unfortunate happened it would be reported because, aside from WatchNet's staff, the people who were watching were the public themselves. You got credit for monitoring, extra for reporting, jackpot for information that led to a criminal conviction. The world was our Neighbourhood Watch. And it worked, too, to a reasonable degree anyway. Sure, if you really want to harm someone else you can always find a way, but the levels of casual crime were tiny compared to, say, those of Elodie's youth fifty odd years ago.

I paused the looping video of No Secrets.

If you wanna see mine, she'd been signing. *I wanna see yours. All of it. All of it. Fucking all of it. No secrets!*

I found it difficult to sympathise with her anger. No one had ever been going to strip the public completely of their privacy. If anything, now, your private things were more private. There were clear lines. As long as you observed them, you were fine. So what if we all had to be on all the time these days? To pay more attention to our appearance and watch our P's and Q's a bit more, under the gaze of family, friends, schools, bosses, colleagues, clients... All watching, judging, catching your every slip of the tongue or unguarded roll of the eyes. It wasn't even just about your proticks or perticks – your aggregated professional and personal standing in the world that influenced everything from employability to the chances of getting a date. It was all about being a better public person. A small price to pay for a safer world.

Right about then, I became aware of a not unpleasurable but wholly inappropriate sensation. Through the eyes of bees I watched myself crossing my legs, smoothing the hem of my skirt over my knee.

"You get paid after the favour, you bastard. Not before." Only a high end liptracer could have made that out through my smile. "Cut it out."

"Make me." Pawel's eyes brimmed with challenge and the sensation trebled.

I uncrossed my legs again, folded my hands in my lap instead. In my face I opened up a ware suite, checked connectivity, pushed a slider up to maximum, and was rewarded by the fact that his eyes actually crossed for a second. If he was going to make me regret giving him the login to my wireless piercings, he wasn't going to have it all his own way.

Anyone dropping in on WatchNet's feed from *Quai St Michel* that afternoon would have seen nothing more than a smartly attired business woman carefully not drinking her second beer. If that wasn't professionalism, I didn't know what was.

Two

"Seriously? There's nothing?" I'd just got back to Bradford. Some people still claimed you had to move away from your hometown to maximise those proticks, but in my line of work I wasn't at all convinced it made any difference. Half the time your physical location was the last thing people needed to know. It wasn't as if they couldn't hear the Yorkshire in my accent wherever I happened to be.

It was raining as I walked up from the station and it felt as if I'd been away for weeks. Out of habit, but without expectation, I skimmed through the footage of my empty flat. I live sparsely. The public rooms of my Homespace are an exemplar of simple, tasteful living with enough quirky, humanising items thrown in to convince clients that I'm someone they can work with. Nothing was out of place. I checked my ticks too. They were slightly up, and I wondered if word was getting out about the Eagles memoir. It was a little early for a swell of interest, but I wasn't about to turn my nose up at it, even if to capitalise on it meant being seen to be working industriously and conspicuously late for a while.

"Nothing at all?" Pawel never failed to come through. The

net never lost anything. The Way Back Machine had begun as an earnest novelty before Elodie was born, but since then it had become an industry in its own right.

"Technically, there's nothing." He was using his ju-ju to piggyback a bee somewhere, but it was too close to him to tell where. There was background noise and the image was shaky, then he went dark for ten, fifteen seconds. A tunnel. He was on a train. Something happened when the light came back, a momentary blurring of his face. I knew better than to mention it, but it distracted me.

"Fizz?"

"What?"

"So, I was telling you about this hole?"

"Right. In the information?"

"Uh-huh. Look at this."

The document he sent me was a cached version of an ancient media message board entitled: NOSX. I saw immediately that the contents went way beyond what you'd expect from music fans gathering to adore their idols. "Where did you get this?"

Pawel's voice dropped to a whisper, his lips barely moving. "I've got a contact who collects old police hardware. The box this came from used to be a backup server in Edinburgh."

It was easy to see why the authorities had taken an interest. Running through the more usual fannish squee was the rhetoric of violence and revolt. "The wages of mixing entertainment and politics," I murmured. It was an understatement.

Pawel snorted. "This used to be *the* fan-site until the anarcho-activists got involved. The original fans saw it as the desecration of their shrine by a bunch of asshats who cared nothing for the music. The flame-wars were epic."

"Yeah, but Elodie didn't condone any of that, did she?"

"Come on, Fizz. Have you actually listened to her songs? She was on lists belonging to every police force in Europe. They wouldn't let her on a plane heading anywhere remotely in the direction of America."

"But she still didn't actually come out and say..." I stopped, annoyed at myself. I used to have a shred of professional impartiality.

"She didn't once decry them either," Pawel said. "There were even rumours on the board that she took part in the organising under an alias."

"Oh, come on..."

"No, really. They all had aliases. There's probably no way to trace most of them after this length of time."

I swallowed my next ugly reply. Bickering wasn't helping. "Okay, you said: a hole. There's nothing on here about the Glasgow gig?"

"Check out the date of the last post."

It had been the day after the show. "So what? They just stopped posting after that gig? They had nothing to say after a night like that? The boot boys weren't crowing, the devotees weren't angry? Okay, maybe a few of them spent a night in the cells or in hospital, but..."

Pawel nodded. "I found some private messages between a handful of the more active *real* fans. Including the moderator." He pulled a grimace. "Someone called *SekritSkwirl*."

"You're kidding."

But he wasn't. Whoever old Sekrit was, the board's original members had been at him for months to close the thing down, but he'd stuck it out claiming loyalty to Elodie's anti-censorship principles. Whatever had transpired in Glasgow, though, had been the last straw.

That's it, the moderator had written in the early hours of the following morning. *It's over, but for those that were there at least it was ours. Our secret. And they can't touch it.*

"That doesn't make sense," I said. "Keeping secrets doesn't sound like something Elodie would have endorsed." And then I saw the paradox. The difference between Elodie-then and Elodie-now. With her self-imposed exclusion from surveillance, she was anything but open. What had caused this about-face? This fabled gig took on another layer of mystery.

Pawel went on: "Two days later the band announced the split formally."

"We need to find out why," I said. "But how are we going to do that if we only have aliases?" Pawel didn't answer. He had been distracted by voices from further down his train. I looked on the other bees but they had drifted into other carriages. "I said, we need to find out –"

Pawel faced me again and there was something sparky in his eyes. "No time, Fizz," he said, as another document appeared in my face. "I ran a lifestyle analysis of the fans that lived in a four hundred mile radius at that time and did some account cracking. Blog postings, social network statuses, favourites lists, media purchases, political histories, criminal records. These are the ones that *should* have been there; the ones with a big silent hole in their histories for that day and the days that followed. Pay special attention to the one at the top. I'd bet he's got the nuts." He glanced away again. The voices were getting louder.

"What's going on?" But he had broken the connection.

A second later an audio file started playing. Angry guitars, harsh electronics, screams. It was another HitMEBritney's track. Another, presumably intentionally contrary, take on the erosion of the old privacy laws, *Outta My Garden*.

The voices on the train had had the ring of officialdom, so I decided that Pawel had a good reason for such an abrupt farewell, but it was difficult not to feel slighted.

> *Stay outta my garden. Don't trample my rose.*
> *Stay out of my business or I'll cut off your nose.*

I was beginning to realise that Pawel might harbour more than a small amount of sympathy with some of the politics of Elodie Eagles.

I stepped out of Glasgow's Central Station into a street that was close to deserted by people, but swarming with bees. The air between these ornate Victorian office buildings was black with their constant gyre. You couldn't blame the locals for staying out of sight. Anyone might feel as if so much scrutiny was certain to find them guilty of something.

When I asked the veteran behind the wheel of my taxi, he was only too happy to enlighten me. "It's the City Council, hen," he said. "Got a fine tradition of spying in place of getting the polis to do a day's work. They were first to fire up the old Big Brother poles on every blimmin' street corner. First to stick body cameras on the civic patrols. Got a blimmin' European grant to be first to introduce bees into a British city. And now look at the place. It's no' just the WatchNet bees here. There's polis bees, traffic bees, litter bees fer chrissakes. And they claim we've the lowest inner city crime rates in the Europe? It's no bloody wonder. No bugger comes here for fear of getting fined for picking their nose."

He dropped me somewhere in the West of the city with a dour wave and an address to ping when I wanted him to return. A chilly breeze blew between the stilted legs of the apartment block. It carried spray from the glittering river beyond, the water a Mediterranean blue that belied its industrial heritage. It must have cost a bomb. A shining example of both tailored algae technologies and misplaced priorities.

I found the entrance partially hidden by the tail of a vertical garden that had been left to its own devices. I might have been looking all day if a neighbour hadn't exited through the low hang of the foliage. I caught the door before it shut, then sought out the apartment.

The resident knew who I was right away. "I told you," he said through the closed door. "I don't talk to journalists."

"No you didn't." I would have been annoyed if his behaviour in our spectacularly unproductive relationship so far had not been so reassuringly reminiscent of Elodie. "And I'm not a journalist."

"Well, whatever you are, can you not take a hint"? The muffled voice was snappish but, I thought, fearful too. "I never answered your messages because I have nothing to say to you scum. Now, piss off."

"Mr Templeton," I persisted. "Gordon. I'm not a journalist. As I mentioned in my messages, I've been hired by Elodie Eagles to write her memoir. I did attach a copy of the contract."

Silence. A chink of uncertainty.

"Gordon, I'm doing this for Elodie. She needs help."

After a further pause, the door swung open.

Gordon Templeton's flat wasn't a home, it was a bunker. I passed through low-hanging curtains of sparkwire in the dim hallway; the microcurrents made my skin crawl and there were dead drones on the carpet inside the entrance. There was stuff everywhere. As I edged around a wall of car batteries I saw plastic-wrapped pallets of bottled water and slabs of tinned food in the darkened kitchen.

"Expecting an apocalypse any time soon?" It slipped out, but at least I wouldn't have to worry about being observed here.

"Think you know everything, you people." Gordon Templeton was an old man. He was probably no more than five years older than Elodie, but age had leached him. His hair was greasy grey, unkempt; his gait stiff; posture within his Greenpeace tee-shirt and joggers compressed by the weight of his worries. "Apocalypse, you call it? Well, I don't know about that, but something's coming right enough."

I did get irritated then. With Templeton for losing touch with the world so obstinately; with Elodie for filling his head with her angsty teenage dramas, snaring them there with her passion and then growing up and moving on. You wouldn't catch her living in a survivalist shelter now.

Templeton's living room was a museum of stupid machines, the kind that needed wires to power and connect them. They were stacked into towers against the walls and connected to an enormous screen. With the steel plating across the windows, the only illumination in the room came from the multitude of power lights, a profusion of red, amber, green, electric blue, some dim, some dazzling, winking slowly or rapidly like evening fireflies. I said a *museum*, but that's wrong: the place was a mausoleum for obsolescence. Pawel would have loved it.

Templeton slumped onto a sofa that itself was in the advanced stages of collapse, dislodging an empty tuna can as he fumbled for the handset that woke the screen up. A news service was showing highlights of the day's politics from across Europe. The feature cut to a face that had recently become familiar. Angela Hardwick was an MEP from the South East with a hard-on for access to the personal information of suspected criminals and she'd been pushing something called the Use Of Private Data Bill for months now. It seemed it was slowly gaining traction among her peers.

"Fucking leech." Gordon Templeton spat on the floor and changed the channel. Instantly, the screen was filled by an image of Elodie. It wasn't a flattering shot, clearly a frozen moment from a live performance, but you could really see the youthful anger beneath the sweat. And there was something else too. In her eyes, a fragile bewilderment that I realised was at the core of everything she had become. She was what, nineteen, by this point? She was a child, asking: *Why is the world like this? Why isn't anyone doing anything to stop it?*

"Are you SekritSkwirl?" I asked as I sat beside him.

"No." He sighed, then added: "Not for a long, long time, hen. You said she needed help."

I looked at him now. "Gordon, she has Alzheimers. She's forgetting what it all meant."

"We're all getting old, hen," he said, but without venom now. He was staring at the screen. "Those days are long gone."

I nodded at Elodie's image. "But you have this to remind you."

His fingers squeezed the remote and frozen Elodie snapped

into action with a deafening blare. The shot cut away to John Eagles hunched over laptops, module racks and a patch-lead-festooned analogue rig, sweating out sweeping squeals and near subsonic bass pulse. A wobbly amateur pan over to the drummer, slicing and dicing the rhythm on his cymbals like he was juggling knives.

"That was the guy that had died. Dave Fenton?" I was wondering again what it was that had caused Elodie to sack her band that night. Had they made the mistake of trying to rein in the anarcho-queen?

"She was better off without him. Without them both."

It took a moment for Templeton's words to sink in. The band had clearly been a proper unit, and after the Britneys Elodie's career had faltered. By all accounts, the solo efforts and subsequent other bands had been more commercial, but they'd lacked the raw engagement. Even when she had been reunited with John Eagles the results were a shadow of the original work, and not even the most ardent fan could have put his hand on his heart and said otherwise.

"Gordon, what happened that night here in Glasgow?"

He looked away, boosted the volume of the television a couple of notches. The shot was back to Elodie now, kneeling on her guitar, thumping the strings with a fist, other hand gripping the microphone like a weapon.

"Gordon…?"

"I don't know what you mean."

I took the remote from him, froze Elodie once more, this time in a tableau more of despair than fury. "Listen to me," I said. "That gig. That night. I know something really important happened. Something that changed everything." He was shaking his head, as if by doing so my words could not enter his ears. "Elodie knows something happened, but she can't remember it. For her it's gone. Do you understand what I'm saying?" At last he looked at me; hope-tinged suspicion. "It doesn't have to go in the memoir. But please, for her."

"All right, if it'll get shot of you I'll tell you what I tell every other persistent fucker that's turned up here asking about that," he said. "It was just for the fans. The real fans. Not the arseholes who spoiled everything. It was just for us. Fuck the politics. Fuck the world. It was just about the music."

"So, what happened?"

"Nothing," he said. "It was a gig. She sang songs. We listened. That was it."

"Do you expect me to believe that?"

The old boy shrugged in answer.

"Gordon, they sent armed police in. There were running battles."

"So you say."

"So, everyone says..." I realised that I was raising my voice, and forced myself to dial it back. "What about pictures, footage."

The old man's face was grey in the light from the screen, but the tear tracks were bright as mercury. He shook his head again.

"There must be something I can take back to her, Gordon."

Templeton dabbed at his cheeks with bear-like paws. "Tell her..." he said. "Tell her she changed our lives. Tell her thanks and tell her we understood. That the Panopticon was never going to happen."

Three

On the train back to Yorkshire I had a great deal of frustration to vent. Templeton had been the fan group's self-appointed documenter-in-chief. He'd have snapped an envelope if it had Elodie's name on. People like that can't help themselves. I resented his lack of trust. If I promised any footage he gave me was to be for Elodie's use only, I bloody well meant it.

I couldn't raise Pawel, so instead I left a not-so-carefully-worded message for him that elicited a few tuts from my fellow passengers and likely from anyone watching through the bees as well. There were times when the pressure of being always on my guard got even to me, though I still wouldn't have traded the occasional opportunity to swear extravagantly in public for the safety that blanket surveillance had brought to our society.

The second I finished, another call came through. I answered immediately, only registering too late that it was my mother.

"Your Auntie Jackie's left that fucking waster, hasn't she."

Instinctively I cupped my hand over my ear bud and scanned for any bees close enough to have picked up the overspill of her uncouthness. This was the kind of conversation I preferred to have in my PL'd bedroom. Actually, every conversation with Mum fell into that category. She was of Elodie's generation, but instead of railing against the changes occurring in her world, she'd accepted them. She'd never worried too much about privacy anyway. In fact some might use the term *exhibitionist*. She didn't deny that, and challenged anyone who had a problem with it. I kept my expression blank, nodded attentively and tried to make my end at least sound like a business call. "Well, that's not unexpected. Thanks for letting me know."

"Not unexpected? It's the third time since October. Rhian, she's well shot of that twat."

"Oh, you think this is a permanent move?" I didn't add: *this time*.

"You know what she's like, that one. Up and down like a yo-yo –"

"Well that sounds positive anyway –"

"Is that all you've got to say about it?"

"For now, yes. I think that'll do it. Thanks again. I'll call you later for an update."

I cut the call, sat back in my seat with a sigh and counted the fact that I'd kept the conversation to under a minute as one of my successes of the week. Even if it did mean I'd committed to the full ordeal later on.

I spent the rest of the journey trying to flesh out Elodie's memoir, but I couldn't concentrate. In the end I achieved little more than blocking in the outline, lining up a selection for the video segments and leaving space for the voiceover text that I'd get around to writing soon. But I found it impossible to go any further without knowing what really happened at that gig. Which was it – the night she'd stoked the fires of revolution, or the night she'd admitted defeat?

In the end I called her Homespace. I wasn't certain she would answer, but she did so instantly, looking up at her living room camera, curled up cat-like, on the same sofa I had eaten *longues-du-chat* on a week before. She wore pyjamas and a diva's silk robe. Her hair was frizzed and she wore no make-up, but she still managed to affect that cocksure pout when she greeted me. "Miss Fitzgerald?"

On impulse I decided that I was done with pussy-footing. "What's Panopticon?"

A comic scowl. "Now who's been telling you about that?"

"A little squirrel. Although, that was about *all* he said."

Instead of replying, Elodie leaned forward to get her cigarettes from the little table. The concentration apparent in the way she slipped an individual cigarette out of its cellophane skin, snapped off the self-igniting cap and took a long, eyes-closed draw to get it going, made me wonder if she'd heard me. Then she reached forward once more, tapped her ash off into the beautiful glass bowl and, as she settled back again, gave a brittle cough that made her face pucker in a way that spoke of other ailments in addition to the Alzheimers.

"It's frustrating when people keep things from you, isn't it?" she said. I snorted. Was this some kind of game? I had a mind to show her what happened when you pushed my buttons, but then she went on. "But that's the price of our society. The more intrusion we have, the more information we make available in the public domain, the greater the sense of entitlement to see more. Be honest with me, when you visited here, you were frustrated because you felt entitled to be able to broadcast yourself in my home."

I cleared my throat, composed myself. "Your feelings are not so uncommon," I said with what I considered to be an astonishing amount of tact, and then with decidedly less, added, "among the older generation."

"Perhaps," Elodie said around her cigarette. "We were all about personal space when I was young. And you're correct of course. Even back then we knew there was never a chance of abolishing surveillance. Our society would just have to learn to live with it or ride it out until the next paradigm kicked us in the teeth."

"Which would be?"

Her shrug would have been elegant if it had been less stiff. In effect it was like watching Young Elodie and Old Elodie fighting for control of the same body.

"Who knows?" she said. "Who ever knows? Back then we thought it would be when this socialised snooping was carried through to its logical conclusion. When everyone could find out anything and there could be no secrets. We called it Panopticon. You can always trust the Greeks for a cool name."

I tried not to smile. The idea was so naïve that even Gordon Templeton had rejected it. "There will always be secrets, Elodie." It was talking to someone in a care home. "There will always be privacy. There has to be."

She pointed her cigarette at the camera. "You're very trusting, Miss Fitzgerald. That's the curse of your generation."

I ignored that. "So that's what Panopticon was? That's what your fans were protecting?" I tried to keep my voice free of scorn, but failed. "A rallying cry amongst your anarchist geeks –"

"A song," she said. "Panopticon was a song, an idea set to music. Nothing more."

"Could I get a copy of this song?" I already knew what she was going to say.

"I never wrote it down, and to my recollection – which admittedly is not to be wholly trusted, but I'm certain of this – I only played it one time."

"In Glasgow?"

She raised an eyebrow, took a long draw and released it, then nodded.

My foul mood lasted until the taxi dropped me outside my apartment block, and when I went to my Homespace it got a whole lot worse. There were people in my house. A man and a woman, seriously dressed, waiting. Even as I wondered why

Homespace had not alerted me, I already knew. There are only a handful of authorities that could legally override your home privacy settings.

I broadcast my voice to my kitchen. "Can I help you?"

Both of their heads snapped up, looked straight at the camera in the corner of the room. "Ah, Miss Fitzgerald," they said. "If could just join us upstairs, we'd like a word."

The word was a boulder. Hard, heavy and impossible to swallow. The woman delivered it when I came through the door. It rolled from rigid lips, a fissure in a stony face. Her voice rumbling on, unstoppable; all the while her partner was speaking too, a tumbling scree that portended worse to come.

"What's he saying?" In a panic I scanned for bees, and saw that there were two in the room. One circling slowly at ceiling height, the other hovering closer, level with the visitors' heads.

"Just your rights and various other pieces of legal boilerplate. Your acceptance is assumed. If you really feel the need, you can listen to them separately on playback. Now, do you –"

"Why's he reading my rights? Who are you? What are you doing here in my home? People will see."

"Miss Fitzgerald... Rhian." Her voice had an Ulster twang. Her solid hand on my arm stopped me talking, made me drop my overnight bag. "No one will see. This dwelling has been appropriated by the Criminal Investigation Department of Police England for the duration of this private interview. Do you understand?"

I nodded. Anyone dropping in on my apartment – family, friends, customers – would not see this. The relief plummeted instantly into anguish. They'd see nothing, except maybe a police advisory notice. My ticks would be tumbling.

"Miss Fitzgerald." The woman's voice was calm. The man had shut up at last and I was able to concentrate on what she was saying. "The faster you answer our questions, the sooner you can get back to your life." She waited until she was certain that I was up to speed and then she started again.

"Do you know a person who calls himself Matts Jansen?"

"No."

"How about Howard Selby? Merljyn deVries? Jonatan Keller?"

I shook my head at each name. "I don't understand. Who are these people?"

"Person. Jansen is wanted for questioning by numerous European agencies. Of course, you may know him by yet another name."

My face popped on then. Unbidden. I actually gasped in surprise. "What –?" Files were opening and closing in a blur of colour and image, audio overlaying audio, babel-like.

The sense of invasion made me physically sick.

"What are you doing? You can't – Are you arresting me?"

The woman sighed. "As my colleague has already explained, you are under data arrest. Until you are otherwise informed, your personal and business files, as well as ongoing communications, are open to investigation. Anything we find in your files that might be of use to our investigation, we can remove copies of. You won't be able to edit or delete any existing files for a while but otherwise you remain at liberty to carry on with your life as normal."

"Who is Pawel?" It was the first time the man had spoken directly to me. He had a sour mouth.

"Pawel Sisic," I said, disconcerted. Not wanting to betray anything. "He's my friend."

"Just a friend?" A video came to the top of the image pile. Me, on my bed, in a state of partial undress and obvious arousal. I was moaning Pawel's name. Another one, same scene, different night. And another, this time a different bed. A hotel somewhere. There were a lot of videos. Sometimes, I got a kick out watching myself. I didn't consider that it made me a deviant. Defiantly, I closed them down.

"A boyfriend then," I said. "No, not that. A *fuck-buddy*." There was more invective in that than I intended. I'd never have been so coarse if I hadn't been certain no one was watching, but now I got some small satisfaction seeing my interrogators raise an eyebrow.

"Is this him?" The woman again. A new video appeared. A man, tall, in his thirties, getting off a bus somewhere in Eastern Europe. I'd never seen him before, but it didn't mean that it wasn't Pawel. Either his real face, or yet another digital mask

"No," I was able to say with almost complete honesty.

"Okay." The image vanished. "Tell us everything you know about the Panopticon Project."

The change of gear surprised me once again, but it was a relief at least to be able tell them something. It didn't take long to relate my involvement with Elodie Eagles, what I'd discovered about her fans and their old idealisms. How, as far as I knew, the Panopticon Project was a fifty year dead dream.

The man grunted. The woman cracked a smile.

"Don't know much, do you, Miss Fitzgerald?"

I didn't know whether it was meant to be offensive or not, but they were already making their way to the door.

"One last thing." My breath of relief got trapped half-in, half-out. "Isn't it a bit funny that there are no pictures, no contact details, no evidence at all in fact of your boyfriend – pardon me, your *fuck-buddy* – anywhere in your files?"

The woman inclined her head in a smirk. "Our address is on your desktop. Do us a favour and ask this Pawel to get in touch, will you?"

They were gone, but they weren't really gone and I didn't know if they would ever leave me alone again. I wanted to call Pawel, but knew that this DI Muldoon and her friend would be waiting for me to do exactly that.

I made tea and tried to work, to pull together the threads of Elodie's life into a script, but I just couldn't. I looked up the news and found that it was dominated once again by Angela Hardwick, restating her claim that a more open data regime across the continent was going to make it much more difficult for criminals and idealogical antagonists to operate in, not to mention on a domestic level protecting things like personal banking and medical insurance by limiting the exposure to private risk. Your data was safest when it was being monitored, she argued. In my present circumstance, I found it hard to agree. I checked my messages and, finding nothing, wondered if it was possible that the police were syphoning off Pawel's attempts to contact me, felt abandoned because it was far more likely that there simply weren't any. He'd keep at a safe distance until he was certain it was safe to contact me again. If it ever was.

It was when I looked in the junk filters that I found seven identical messages, sent on the hour from a company called *Magic Moments*. They were data skimmers, dressed up fancy but skimmers nonetheless. Stuff like this was the most common form of spam in my profession. Normally I ignored them, but sometimes I dipped in to see if there were any ideas worth stealing. That day I just needed the distraction.

The voices of Maurice Chevallier and Hermione Gingold swelled in my ear bud. *We met at nine. We met at eight.* A couple walking in a leafy autumnal parkscape. A voiceover, male, American, insincere, going on about all the memories that fade into misremembrances when you lose your files, how *Magic Moments'* team of skilled data miners can return those moments to you...

I selected the whole lot for deletion, but there was something about the couple that stayed me. I watched them sit on a bench overlooking a duck pond. The camera swung around over their shoulders, zoomed in as the man put his arm around the woman.

"Do you remember where we first met, darling?"

The woman I thought looked a bit like me. The man – there was no mistaking it – was the person I knew as Pawel.

I put on my coat, bustled through the kitchen to pick up a

loaf of bread which had staled during my recent absence, and left the flat in what I hoped didn't look like too much of a hurry.

It was a nippy afternoon, overcast and glowering, so I had no problems finding a bench near the Queen's centenary pond. I parked myself there, slowly tearing corners off the bread and tossing them onto the water where the ducks swam apathetically close to investigate.

Did I remember where we met? Well it wasn't at a duck pond, that was for certain. I kicked off an MMO I used to be somewhat obsessed with, and still revisited on occasion when I wanted to get away from things for a while. *Chalice*, it was called. The standard old heroic swords and wizardry fare that had never really gone out of fashion.

On hearing the first strains of the introductory music, I smiled. On the first sight of my kick-ass rat warrior avatar, whiskers twitching, fur lustrous, black eyes glittering, I smiled a little more. If the police had a profile for me this would be bang in the centre of my behavioural bell curve. But comfort gaming was not the point of this exercise. And even if they suspected the ulterior motive for my sudden return to the gameworld today, they'd have difficulty following me to my assignation. There were two ways of getting to where I was going: several months of serious gameplay or sequestering GM assistance, and since Pawel was a silent partner in the company it was anyone's guess which of those routes would be the quicker.

On the bench, I was aware of a bee drowsing by – a real one, which was surprising so early in the year. I shivered, buttoned my coat and pulled my scarf up around my neck, over my chin. All the better to foil liptracers.

"You take the girls to all the swanky places."

The golden dragon raised itself into a sitting position on the little outcrop that rose from the centre of the lake of fire. It turned its regal head towards me.

"I knew you'd remember," Pawel said.

"How could I forget? It's not every day you fall for someone

33

you meet in Hell. Although, this..." I scanned my surroundings. The basalt pebbles skittered under my furry claws, the lake boiled, the souls screamed, but it seemed less impressive than I remembered.

The dragon grinned. "Private instance for just the two of us. Technically it's not attached to the gameworld. Technically, it's on a different server on a different continent, and it moves every few minutes. If anyone tried to follow you here through Chalice, they'd be in a different Hell to us now."

"Technically?"

"Technically."

Now that I knew that it was safe to talk I found I didn't know what to say, because the next words I spoke would give voice to my suspicions and destroy the comfortable half-anonymity we'd enjoyed for so long. But I needed to hear his side of it.

"You know the police came to see me?"

"I saw."

"You were watching on police-appropriated bees?"

The dragon smiled sheepishly. "Such things are possible."

"Uh-huh. And while we're on the subject of your snooping skills, have you been tidying up in my files?" The police were right, there certainly should have been plenty of embarrassing videos of Pawel. I didn't know if I was annoyed or grateful. I looked at the big reptilian head, thought about Pawel's own face, about how it had always suited me to ignore the tiny glitches and pixilations.

"I'm sorry," he said. "The masking only applies to my face. Distinguishing features and all that."

For now I was less worried about moles and birthmarks than I was about the reason for all this. "Those names. The men they are after. Are they you?"

The dragon's head swayed from side to side in a non-committal gesture. "Not really."

"And is *Pawel* really you?"

"It is for now. What can I say, Fizz? It's complicated."

"Do I want to know? Do I want to be involved?"

"I'm sorry, but you're already involved."

My rat held her forepaws up, acknowledging that it had been a stupid thing to say. "Look, just tell me... Is it legit?"

The dragon laughed, giving out a series of smoke puffs. "You mean, am I a bad man?"

I made my rat princess slap the side of her head in a *well, duh* action.

When he answered, his tone was a measure more serious. "You know I operate at a government level? Well, the relative goodness of the work I do really depends on who's paying for it. But generally..." Dragons shouldn't shrug. There are limits to anthropomorphism.

"Generally...?"

"I believe I'm fighting on the side of the righteous."

My rat princess blinked at him. "Am I in danger? My mum...?"

"No one's life is in danger, I promise. Look, I'll see what I can do to make the charming Donna Muldoon lose interest in you. The best thing for you to do is resume life as normal and carry on with your work. Find out about the Glasgow gig and get that memoir written."

I snorted. "How? Elodie can't tell me what happened. Gordon Templeton won't..."

The dragon's grin was all Pawel. "I think I might be able to help you there. If you're up for trying something a little unorthodox."

Tentatively, at first, the rat grinned back.

I trudged home in prickling rain, hoping to hide the confidence I'd taken from my conversation with Pawel. The familiarity of the Chalice environment fed a strong need in me to believe in him. It didn't assuage the more general doubts the visit from the police had, if not created then certainly amplified, but it was something. By the time I was back inside, however, I knew that something wasn't enough. We'd agreed to meet in Chalice again after whatever it was he was sending arrived. I told myself I could put off making any kind of judgement until then.

I tiptoed through my own rooms. The rainclouds outside created a tomb-like gloom but I didn't want wake the lights for fear of activating dormant bees. They were such a common sight – most often resting on windowsills to recharge, the jointed form with its smoked plastic camera head and the barrel-shaped powerpack with WatchNet's distinctive pair of slender orange stripes, the flimsy rotors folded away until needed for flight – that the tendency was to overlook them, but now I looked for the little spies and I looked hard. As far as I could tell there were none. Nevertheless I locked myself in the bathroom before I sat down to call my mother.

"You'll have to be quick, Rhian. I'm late for work." She was talking via her Homespace rather than her face. The room mics flattened her voice. The image from her cluttered hall as she checked her make-up and hair in the mirror was blurred. I was fairly certain that the lenses in her cams had never been given so much as a wipe in the seventeen years she'd lived there.

"Oh, okay." I tried not to feel annoyed that on the one occasion that I needed to talk to her, she didn't have time for me. I failed. "Which one is it today?"

Mum opened a button on her shirt, adjusted her cleavage and I knew, even before she said: "Just the Belles, love." *The Belles' End* was one of a number of dodgy bar jobs mum worked, a men's rights segregationist pub of the type that no one with any sense approved of but apparently had to be allowed to exist for reasons of equality as long as no one else's rights were being infringed in the process. How expecting my mother to dress like someone out of a 1970s television comedy wasn't infringing her rights was beyond me, but her proticks weren't high enough to get better work. Something, for example, with health insurance or a pension. Her perticks, on the other hand, fluctuated like a yo-yo, depending on what she'd done most recently and who was watching at the time. Her name occasionally appeared on some really insalubrious charts too: Bradford's Top Barmaids, Yorkshire GILFS, trash like that. I'd been forced to change my name for professional reasons. Building my business had been difficult enough without the catastrophic drain any association with my mother would have on my ticks.

Nevertheless, I needed to talk to her now, and I didn't know how to start.

"You've got four minutes before I'm out of here." Mum went through to the kitchen where the camera view was just a smear of cooking grease. I hopped onto WatchNet on the off chance there were any bees in her place. There were several, and the first one I tried was hovering over her bed. The sheets were on the floor and a naked middle-aged man lay sprawled and snoring. His flesh was doughy, his face worn and in sleep almost innocent. There was a comment thread attached to the feed that stretched back the last hour and, even without reading it, made me feel sick.

"Mum." I bounced to a bee in the kitchen instead. She was scraping jam onto toast. "You've got to be more careful..." She didn't even disguise her sigh. We'd had this conversation so many times. She marched through to the bedroom and laid the plate of toast beside the sleeping stranger, then looked directly at the floating bee.

"Time's up, chick. Call you later."

I didn't know what more I'd expected. I'm not saying that Helen Marsden never showed me an ounce of mother's love. She did, freely and plentifully, but we didn't see eye to eye on so many things that it had become impossible to actually converse. She gossiped about friends and family and sniped at what she saw as my overly cautious approach to life. I in turn criticised and chided. I wondered for the first time in ages whether it was me, whether being so mindful of how you appeared to others might be a stupid way to live after all. But if you wanted to get anywhere in a world where everybody had an opinion about you, what other option could there be?

I wished I could work, but it felt as if my files – and I acknowledged the irony that most of my data had once been someone else's data – were tainted by the police's interest. And I felt paralysed by the thought that any movement I made was subject to observation and scrutiny in a way that it had never been before. I checked my inbox for sign of Pawel's promised aid but there was nothing, not even among the junk.

My despondency was interrupted by a visitor alert. My first reaction, fear, evaporated some when I saw that it was a boy struggling with a huge bouquet of flowers. I okayed him up and relieved him of his burden. It was an off-the-shelf assortment, but beautiful nevertheless and dominated by white lilies, trumpet blossoms nodding. When I released them from their bow and cellophane I discovered the card.

Sorry for putting you through Hell, Fizz.
Hope these set you on the road to enlightenment.

I stared at the card, then at the flowers. If this was Pawel's idea of *help*… I examined the card more closely, surreptitiously as a spy would in a movie, for hidden chips or mag strips, but it was just cardboard. I found a vase and transferred the blooms to it one at a time, but there was nothing hidden among the stems and foliage either. For the benefit of any watchers, I made a show of arranging the flowers and it was only when I stepped back to admire my work that I saw it. A bee, a real one, fat and fuzzy, crawling drowsily from inside a lily. It dropped to the table and slowly flexed its legs, shivered its wings and then righted itself. Then it looked right up at me and I knew, as I stared at those impenetrable eyes, as I realised that its fuzz was just too uniform, its stance too symmetrical, that it came from the uncanny valley of made things. Mindful that everything I did at the moment was being monitored, I left the bee to its own devices and, smiling as if delighted by my flowers, filled the kettle. While it boiled I tried to act normal: checked my messages, feeds and ticks on my Homespace. Opened up WatchNet and logged a few minutes on my neighbourhood trawl. It didn't get me much credit, but it wouldn't harm my pertick aggregate if people saw that I was continuing to do my duty as a good neighbour, whatever else had befallen me today. I could always rely on there being several WatchNet bees patrolling our street, a handful more in the lane out back. Usually there was at least a couple in each apartment in the block. No one liked a lingering peeper, of course, but it was considered neighbourly to log a few seconds every now and then just to make sure that everything was all right.

Once I'd finished my quick tour, I noticed that there were now apparently two bees in my flat. The WatchNet one hovering quietly above the cupboards must have snuck in while I was talking to Mum, and I had no doubts that it was under official control. The other was right in front of me on the table pretending to be a real living thing, and through its camera I watched myself lift kettle to cup to make the tea I now sorely needed.

This had to be Pawel's offer of help, but I had no idea what to make of it. A bee that looked exactly like a real bee. It was more than unorthodox, it was overkill to a ridiculous degree. A work of art really, and had to have been unbelievably expensive to make. I could kind of see the logic: the police would expect access to the feeds of any commercial bees around me and if they became aware of one they couldn't access they'd be suspicious. Conversely, no one would expect a bee to be a bee.

The questions was: what the hell was I supposed to do with it?

My thoughts on the matter were interrupted by a call that overrode my other apps. It had the Police England colophon, and when I answered it I knew with cold certainty that I'd be looking at DI Muldoon.

"I assume you were just getting round to telling us about the flowers, Miss Fitzgerald," she said without preamble. "We know they're from him, even if we can't trace where they were ordered. Classy way to make an apology, even for a scumbag."

I glanced at the flowers with what I hoped now looked like disdain. "I still don't know what you people think he's guilty of, but if he is involved in something bad it's going to take more than a few poxy flowers –"

Her laugh was lathered in condescension. "Come off it, Rhian. Your wee face lit up when you unwrapped them. And, you were just going to put the call through to us, right? Any second now?"

I shrugged. "It hardly counts as getting in touch."

"Uh-huh." Her expression slid into serious. "And what happened when you were in the park?"

"I was… gaming."

She didn't even bother to laugh this time. "Outside? In this weather? Don't insult us, Rhian. We're not stupid. We know he's not contacted you through conventional means, so what are we supposed to think when you go and sit outside in the rain for half an hour? When you can't be found in the gameworld you just moments ago entered?"

"No I was there –"

"Yeah?" The cop's expression was mocking. The eye-flick betrayed that she was reading something. "*Falls of Ivory*? Your last camp in Chalice. Pretty spot. Idyllic. We've had a bot dwarf chipping away at the same rock there for two weeks waiting for you to show. Imagine our surprise when we watched you log in and… you didn't."

"But –"

"We're not fucking around here, Rhian. You don't even know how much trouble you're in. Get him to call us."

I heard short shaky breaths and realised they were mine. I was completely out of my depth at this game, and cursed Pawel for involving me in these things, and in his life. "I can't. He won't do it." I knew this instinctively, Pawel was too savvy to fall into such a simple trap.

"Then you should try your hardest to persuade him, Rhian." The cop's expression softened. "Look, we know what he's like. But can't you at least try? Make the call. Today." Almost as a friendly afterthought, she added: "This is your last warning."

With that she was gone, and I sat at my table until the shakes subsided. Even then I was thinking that I could spin it to my watchers as something personal, a family thing perhaps. I might even gain some sympathy ticks. What I couldn't do was make that call. Even to attempt it might be to betray Pawel, and as angry as I was with him at that moment, I wasn't quite ready to do that yet.

I went back to Glasgow. The train was overcrowded and I shared a table with a couple who'd clearly had a serious falling out. They sat across from each other, simmering, waiting for the bees to drift off long enough to snip and snipe in furious whispers. Fortunately, these episodes were few and far between because there always seemed to be a bee nearby. They both glared at me as if it was my fault, and it probably was.

The venue that had allegedly hosted Elodie's secret gig had been one of a host of live music bars once popular across Glasgow. I'd already researched it, of course, selected a couple of images for my files, some footage of other bands taken around the same time. It had boasted a low ceiling, an even lower stage, a notoriously sticky carpet.

It wasn't much of a lead but, in truth, I didn't have much else.

The usage of the place hadn't changed much in fifty years, only now instead of a live music venue it was a casting bar. The disinterested bar manager who showed me down to the venue had never heard of Elodie and left me to wander around with a warning not to touch any of the stacks of lighting and intaface equipment that crowded in front of the stage where the punters had once stood; the stuff that allowed music acts to perform to whoever tuned to the venue's cast, although whether they got more or less of a global audience than they might have in person in the old days was debatable. Music casts were ten-a-penny, and casting bars charged aspiring artists chasing ticks through the nose to play.

I threaded my way through the racks to the stage, and tried to imagine what it would have been like to be here the night Elodie had played the song she called Panopticon. I was surprised how close the audience would have been to the performers. Little more than a yearning arm's length. Close enough to touch, to share a real emotional connection. Close enough to feel the spirit of community spreading through the press of bodies. I suppressed a shiver at the thought of being confined so close to others. To feel their breath and smell their sweat and feel the brush of an elbow or thigh as someone behind you shifted position for a better view. How many would have crammed in here in? Fifty? Sixty? It couldn't have taken more than a hundred. It would have been awful.

I wondered where Gordon had stood with his camera. He'd have been fairly tall as a younger man but I guessed that he might be respectful of others, so perhaps at the front but to one side. There was a paint-slathered pillar on the left that he could have used to steady his camera arm. And I could just about imagine Elodie right in front of him, twisting out her words with that throaty moan that I'd disliked to begin with but had now settled into me, shredding the steel strings of a borrowed acoustic guitar, providing a rhythmic accompaniment with taps and slaps on the body.

I could almost imagine it all, but all the imagination in the world wasn't going to show it to me for real. Even with Pawel's miraculous bee because, astounding as it was, it was just a bee not a time machine.

Pawel would say I was wasting time at the venue, putting off the work that needed to be done but, even if I had invented the detour for that reason, now I found that it had really helped me to get a feel for where it had all taken place. Before I left the casting bar I did one more thing: I stepped up onto the stage and stood where Elodie must have stood. Imagined the heat of the stage lights, the intense adoration in the faces of the faithful as they mouthed along to songs they knew by heart. All of them, perhaps, knowing or suspecting this would be the last time... All of them in tears by the end.

I looked up and saw, perched on the casting gear, a WatchNet bee. Defiantly, I brushed the tears from my own cheeks, then pinged the cab and went out into Glasgow's swarming streets to meet it.

Four

Gordon Templeton's place had been trashed. As soon as I stepped out of the lift I saw his door ajar and the stink of smoke from it made something inside me clench. I called out a greeting as I entered, but expected no answer and got none. I registered the cairn of dead bees that now lay beneath the sparkwire at the threshold first. Next I saw that the stockpiles of food and water had been plundered, and what remained lay scattered in the hall. And then I saw what had become of his living room. His beloved banks of antique machines had been systematically disassembled, their insides smashed with the claw hammer that lay nearby, and piled on the carpet before being set alight. Miraculously, the fire hadn't spread to the old couch, but the ceiling was thunder-black with soot, the back wall too, and his huge screen was cracked across from the heat. Not even Pawel's acquaintances with their gifts of resurrection could have salvaged anything from the destruction that Gordon had wrought.

And it had to have been him because the fortress door was undamaged. He'd packed his supplies, burned everything else and gone into hiding. This really was the end of the line. Even Pawel hadn't predicted this. And fuck him very much for his smug secrecy and his useless gifts.

I flopped onto Gordon's awful sofa and pulled the plastic box out of my bag. Pawel's bee was curled up inside. Beautiful, useless thing. I hadn't even known exactly what I'd been supposed to do with it when I got here. I'd started to imagine perhaps that if I could find a place to hide it, away from the sparkwire and out of Gordon's line of sight, it would act as my spy in that WatchNet-free zone, maybe even record him watching his blurred and shaky Panopticon gig footage when he thought he was alone. A copy of a copy would have been better than nothing. But that had always seemed a waste of such a sublimely crafted machine.

The bee uncurled then, flexed, investigated the corners of the box. Its feed popped up in my face, ready. "Sorry to have brought you all this way for nothing," I told it, and then on a whim opened the box and reached in to stroke its amazing fuzzy back. The machine responded, immediately blurring its lacy wings and lifting out of reach. "Shit." I watched it whirr around the room and at the same time surveyed the destroyed machines through its newly opened feed as it circled the junk pile. Close up, the damage looked even worse. Torn-out wiring, shattered boards, black and blistered components.

"What the heck did you think you were protecting, Gordon?" I said to myself. "Where did you go?"

And that was when my face went haywire. A riot blossom of motion and sound as media instance after media instance opened and closed. A rippling bee-wing flutter as scene overlaid scene overlaid scene. At first all the instances were the same – this room, from this bee's slowly circling viewpoint and I thought it was malfunctioning, continually restarting its feed, but then I wasn't looking at a stack of wrecked devices any more. I was looking at Gordon's room as it had been on my first visit. Then that scene vanished and it was back to the destruction.

What had that been? A glitch? A rollback to before he left?

That didn't make sense. The bee hadn't been here earlier. Even as I was puzzling this impossibility, the before scene came back, and this time persisted. Gordon's room as it had been, and as the bee circled and looked towards the couch... instead of me sitting there, it was Gordon himself. The old fellow's face sagged with anxiety. His features flickered as some footage played out on his ancient screen, and when the bee circled around I saw that he was watching Angela Hardwick. Then that instance was overlaid and in the next his expression was pulled tight with rage and on the next tour of the screen I saw now a widescreen map, a route traced in red. That instance became Elodie, singing, a big theatre somewhere. Then a map again, a different one, and another, then Elodie, Elodie, Elodie, but never in the place that had become the casting bar, then back to the first map, repeatedly, until the bee had swung around to face the couch again. I had no idea what I was looking at. And it terrified me.

I didn't think. I called Pawel. "What did you send me?"

He was outside. It was overcast and wind was whipping his hair around. The digital masking blurred as it struggled to keep up. "Fizz?" He was out of breath, like he'd been running. "Where are you? We agreed to meet in Hell. This is stupidly risky."

"Yes, of course, *Fizz*." I should have cared about breaking our agreement, but I didn't. "And I repeat, what is this thing? It's impossible!"

Pawel cast around him and then ducked under an overhang of brickwork. A doorway, I thought, although his tamed local drone didn't show enough to be certain. "Ah, you've used the bee?"

"Of course, I've used your bloody bee –"

"Okay, okay..." He cut me off before I could say any more. "I'll be in touch. It'll be okay, I promise."

And he was gone. Sitting in Gordon Templeton's wrecked room, unobserved by the world, I allowed myself a scream of frustration. Then my anger crumbled, and shame seeped in as I realised that he hadn't been concerned about the risk to himself as much as the risk to me. And as soon as that penny had rolled around the rim and finally dropped, the messages began.

At first they came from concerned, disbelieving friends: *Did you know...? Are you aware...? I don't believe it* personally *but, Rhian, it* really *does look like you.* After that it was it was colleagues angry about confidences and clients wanting to discuss liberties taken with their lives' stories, and with their bills too. And then exes brandishing time-stamped midnight sex-tapes: *you said you were at your mother's...*

There were all the times I plagiarised other students work to get the grades I'd built my career on.

There were the times I'd been making love with Pawel but given the access codes to my sex toys to several other people at the same time.

And there were the times my work had turned up something that a client had not expected to see, and the extra security work required to make sure it didn't come to light had seen my fee inflated by fifty percent. They'd all paid without quibbling, and while I'd felt morally ambiguous about it at the time I'd always found a way to justify it to myself. Now the world was screaming extortion.

I had been turned inside out. All my secrets laid bare. My life, all of it, spread out for everyone to see. A lifetime's carefully cultivated façade torn away to reveal me as I really was. A history of missed payments and two-timing, of seedy sexual appetites and emergency gynaecological visits. An existence of ineptitude and scrabbling and deception. Of lies. I was liar, and everyone that knew me, that visited my Homespace or was in my personal or professional circles, anyone that had given me a tick, ever, knew it now because someone had stolen my whole life and published it far and wide.

My notifications continued to explode. I couldn't breathe. My fingers scrabbled at the material of Gordon Templeton's couch. They found a cigarette-burn and worried at it. The fabric shredded as easily as my life just had. For the long minutes all I could think of was who and how and why? This was going way beyond the data that Muldoon and her crony had flipped so casually through the other day. This was every record of me, everywhere.

In the old days, when net anonymity had been an everyday thing, they used to call it *doxxing*. Personal details published as an act of revenge. When the worst thing that you could think of was people knowing who you really were and associating your online behaviour with your actual real life. When the victim was vulnerable it was coupled with threats of rape or death as a means of silencing unwelcome opinions. Doxxing of that type had been made illegal decades ago. Nowadays the depths it could go to were far worse and, under the label *personal terrorism*, it carried a jail term not far off that of murder. As a result, it was rare.

But it had happened to me.

I managed to stir myself to block my calls, but the messages continued to flood into my inbox, getting more and more demanding, and I realised that the only blessing in any of this was that I was in a WatchNet black spot. At least no one was watching my distress, recording it and adding it to my mountain of shame.

I sat there for a long time trying to get my head around how completely my life was ruined. My ticks would be so far through the floor my business was irredeemable, and it was unlikely that I'd ever be employable again in a meaningful way. My friends circle would have shrunk to nothing as people broke ties to avoid being tainted by association. I might have one or two good people left that I could count on, but I wasn't certain that I'd be able to make myself talk to them.

Despite the block, which not even Pawel should have been able to get around, an incoming call animation started to flash. I stared, petrified by yet another layer of intrusion until I remembered that in a spirit of daughterly responsibility I'd put my mum on the exceptions list. I answered. If anyone was entitled to point and laugh, it was her.

But she wasn't laughing. "Rhian, pet? Are you all right?" It was the genuine concern that broke me, and right there on a horrible couch in a squalid Glasgow flat, I went to pieces.

"Mum, what am I going to do?"

For the first time since I was six years old, my mother made all the right noises and said all the right things. She didn't try to brush it off. She let me talk about how I felt, about everything. And then it was her turn. I couldn't remember her ever talking about her life in such a dispassionate and honest way – how it felt to be haunted, hampered, hamstrung by the things she'd done in her youth, to have the level of her life set forever by a few spilled secrets. Things that didn't really matter, but had become millstones nevertheless.

"The thing everyone gets wrong about their secrets," she told me, "is the assumption that they are special. Rhian, pet, most people's failings – those things they think they'd rather die than have people find out about them – are common as muck. Money? Sex? Lies? Who doesn't have those old clothes hanging in their closet?"

I wanted to protest that my secrets weren't common, that I wasn't the same as everyone else, but even I recognised how childishly entitled that would have sounded. If my so-called career had been about anything it had been about tarting things up to publicly deny that fact, but it made it no less true nor easier to accept.

"See the government, with all their snooping? Their greatest trick is claiming they're doing us a favour by letting us keep those things. Like they're worth something. Honestly, most of the time? I don't care if everyone knows my business. No matter how many times it happens."

Again I bit my tongue against blurting out: *But people expect that of you...* It wasn't only out of shame, this time. I realised she meant something else.

"Mum, they did this to you too?"

She was wearing a glittery indigo eye shadow that softened

her grey eyes, but there was a familiar flintiness there. "It doesn't matter," she said. "I really didn't have far to fall, did I?" My inability to answer was all the response she needed. It elicited a smile as comforting as milky tea.

"What can we do?" I said.

She arched a carefully drawn eyebrow. "Well, as soon as my shift is over I'm planning to get spectacularly off my tits on the cheapest wine this place serves and then find someone to escort me home and bang me until my legs fall off and just say *fuck you* to the lot of them. You'd be welcome to join me, but I don't think that'd be your style, love."

I smiled, shook my head.

"What I'd do if I were you? I'd get away somewhere for a few days and think about what's important in your life. It's never over, pet. Not while you've still got breath."

When she'd gone I realised that she hadn't asked who had done this. Likely she didn't think it mattered if it was a random attack or someone I'd managed to piss off somewhere along the line. What was done was done, right? What must she have imagined I'd done to deserve this, though? I didn't have any enemies. At least I didn't think I did. The only time I'd been remotely threatened lately was by DI Muldoon. She'd never given me an *or what* when she'd said I had one more chance to get Pawel to call her, but... The police wouldn't do something like this, surely? And the only person I knew with the actual skills to pull off something like this was Pawel himself, and that made even less sense.

The not knowing was almost as bad as the act itself.

I knew one thing for certain. Even if the police were not involved in my exposure, they would want to know who was and use it as leverage to make me give up Pawel. They would be watching on the bees, waiting for me to emerge from Gordon's flat. And then they would follow me home on the train, and hound me everywhere I went after that. Who knew how long it would go on for. Suddenly, getting away somewhere sounded like a really good plan. In my face I rolled the bee's feed back to the image of Gordon's map, the route arrowing north and west out of the city, into the mountains and wilderness.

I probably had no reason to continue with Elodie's memoir. The chances were high that somewhere in that still-growing flood of messages, she had already dissolved our contract. If only it could be as simple to uncover her lost secrets as it apparently was to display mine to the world...

Then it hit me: I didn't have enemies, but what if Elodie did? Political ones that would stop at nothing to prevent that gig footage from coming to light? Despite both Elodie and Gordon's assurances that it had just been about the music, the camaraderie of friends who'd come to mark the ending of something they'd loved and shared... Hadn't Gordon mentioned that other people had come asking about the gig?

Well, whoever it was, it worked. As sources went, I couldn't be any more discredited. Which meant that it didn't matter what I did now. Screw them, whatever their reasons. Even if I didn't get to tell Elodie's story now, I was going to keep on trying to find that footage for her.

My instincts told me that all this destruction had been for show. That gig was too much a part of Gordon for him not to have recorded it, and for him not to have taken it with him wherever he had gone. I looked at his map again, frozen in the feed from Pawel's bee. It was an impossibility, something that I couldn't possibly be seeing, but, given that I *did* see, how could it show me something that wasn't real? If nothing else, it was somewhere to go. I memorised the route then closed down the bee's feed. Next, I located the closest on-street car rental and booked a vehicle. I wondered how far the police would be able to follow me into the Scottish wilds before WatchNet's coverage density dropped to zero. My last problem was the bee. It didn't seem inclined to be cooped up in its box again, but when I pushed through the tingly sparkwire at the door it tagged lazily along, low to the floor. Smart bee, right enough.

Before opening the door, I took a deep breath and whispered a prayer to whoever might be listening for a miracle that might allow me to do this unnoticed. There would be bees out there, and there would be watchers. Maybe not many at first but once someone identified me the word would spread; first person to person and then virally if this went as far as the shaming networks, and it would. I'd become a hot target and WatchNet and the other providers would automatically allocate more resources to follow me. It'd be like living in a cloud of permanent scrutiny. I almost couldn't do it, but somehow I managed to make my arm push the door. The landing and elevator were empty, the ground floor lobby too. Riding my luck, I barged straight outside, through the dangling foliage and into the sunshine... and there were still no bees. The air was fresh and clear and the only sounds I could hear were birdsong, the soft swoosh of vehicles a street away and the unique buzz-tone of my – of *Pawel's* – bee.

I checked the location of my allocated car and ran, soon spotting the dull grey roof in one of the bays ahead. I groaned with relief, but it choked in my throat when I saw a woman approaching from the other direction and climbing into my vehicle. In seconds the car had pulled out of the bay and driven off.

I watched it go, dumbstruck. Of all the luck to be double-booked by a shitty hire company... But that was nothing as shocking as what happened next.

"Sorry, Fizz, it's the best distraction I could arrange." A man with the face that I knew as Pawel was sitting on the bonnet of the car I'd stopped beside. He hadn't been there a second ago, but now here he was – suit, shoes, shit-eating grin, the lot. It took a second to register that he was only there in my face overlay but the effect was still profound.

"They'll be pissed that the local bees all decided to wander off just before you came out, but they'll be satisfied enough that it's you in that car for a while," he said. "But to make it count you have to get going now." He appeared to pat the paintwork of the car he was sitting on. "This belongs to someone called Jean Reynolds. She's on holiday right now, but I'm sure if she knew why you were going to borrow her car she'd be totally fine about it."

"What?" I said. "I can't just take someone's car…"

"I know. What would people think of you? Come on. The password is *weebawbee*, all lower case."

An access window opened in my face. I entered the word he'd given me. It bounced. "Didn't work."

Pawel frowned. "All right, try a variation. Initial caps, separate words, you know the drill."

I tried again, this time splitting the syllables up. The door opened. Pawel clapped his hands and slid off the bonnet. "Sweet. Now, get going. I'll call you in a bit."

I did as he asked, slipping into the comfortable seat as the systems powered on. "Aren't you coming…?"

The door snicked shut on my question, and Pawel was nowhere in sight.

Beginning to consider seriously that I might be having a breakdown, I breathed in and then out as I watched the bee calmly settle on the dashboard and fold its wings as if waiting to for us to be under way.

Well, why not?

I relayed Gordon's route into the navigation and felt the car pull out onto the road. As Glasgow slid soundlessly past me, I found tartan blanket, slouched in the seat and fell asleep. It was the best thing I could have done right then.

The city was gone, replaced by a forest of tall pine trees. The thick trunks trapped light and shadow like secrets. A soft, unfamiliar alert was sounding. It wasn't my face, it was the car.

"Answer," I mumbled and Pawel appeared on the windscreen. I sat up, awake enough to ask: "What the hell is going on?"

"You mean apart from being the most despised fugitive in Europe?" He shrugged. I normally found his flippancy impossibly charming; at that moment it had precisely the opposite effect.

"Don't you do that." Sleep it seemed had distilled my self-pity into rage. "Don't make fun. I stood by you. I *protected* you. You do not get to take the piss out of me for that."

He had the common sense at least to look contrite. "I'm sorry. You're right, and thank you."

I turned away and breathed my anger out, let it mist the window, obscure the trees like fog, then turned back to face him. "Okay, so...?"

"Okay. So?"

"Start with the bee."

"Ah, the bee." Pawel glanced down for a second, working out where to start. "Okay... Well the bee is pretty special."

"You don't say. Special, how?"

"Special in that it talks to other bees."

"You mean it coordinates with WatchNet's bees...?"

"You didn't notice the lack of them when you came out of Templeton's place? I blinked, realising that something had heard my faithless prayer after all. Pawel laughed. "And that's nothing. It's not just WatchNet's bees. Any drones, anything with a quantum brain really, anywhere."

"But there were no other bees in Templeton's flat," I said.

He couldn't help himself. He grinned. And I knew he was going to take his time so that he could enjoy explaining his cleverness to me. "Templeton's vamoosed, right?"

I nodded.

"But imagine –" I opened my mouth to object. "Just imagine, okay? Imagine... that he hasn't."

"But he has."

"But *imagine*. If he'd lingered for a few more days while he made his plans, working out his route, maybe even agonising over whether to leave at all…"

"Okay, I'm imagining." I scowled, still unable to see what he was driving at.

"It could have happened that way? In theory?"

"Sure, I suppose. My visit obviously spooked him, although…" Templeton had mentioned others had come asking about the gig before me. Who was to say there hadn't been more afterwards?

"Exactly. So it's reasonable to assume he got a visit from our friend Muldoon too and that was what spooked him? And if that happened a day or so later rather than sooner, he might not have left yet and, had a bee been present in his flat at the moment in time when you visited earlier it could have recorded his map."

"Wait, what? No! There were no bees. Gordon was a nut for sparkwire…"

"But imagine if he hadn't been quite so security conscious."

"I don't know, maybe? It's possible. All of these things are possible, in theory, but they're not what happened. Gordon is long gone. There was no map, and definitely no bees to film it, and yet I still saw it. How did that happen?"

"I'm telling you how."

"No, you're making me imagine stuff that never happened – "

"Never happened in this universe, Fizz."

"What?"

"The bee talks to other bees on a quantum level. Including other bees in probabilistically congruent universes. Actually, in theory, in all possible universes, but it has most chance of seeing events with the highest probabilities of having happened here."

"Piss off, Pawel." I hated it when he was being ridiculous like this. Unable to bear his face, I turned away again. The trees on my side of the car had thinned and I glimpsed sparkling grey water between them. "Map." Route and terrain blocked Pawel from sight. They told me that the loch, now coming fully into view as the trees dwindled and the road hugged the shore, would be the first in a chain of dramatically picturesque bodies of water I'd encounter before I reached my destination. I'd be a fool to come all this way and not see them. "Clear," I said and all the overlays vanished, Pawel included.

"Don't do this, Fizz." His disembodied voice was about all I could handle of him right now. "Think about it. It makes sense."

I had thought about it, and of course it made sense. If only because no other explanation did. Whether I considered it possible or not seemed to be irrelevant. It was maddeningly logical.

"Fizz? Come on..."

"So, the car." I needed to hear the rest of it. "That was the same thing?"

I heard relief in his voice. "Yes. I did a reccy last week before I sent you the bee. In another universe, Jean Reynolds wasn't on holiday; a bee saw her sitting in the car updating her password."

"But the password didn't work."

That stopped him for a second, and when he replied it was with exasperation. "It was the same password, Fizz. Stop picking nits."

"No," I shook my head. "In that universe it was different. Very similar but not exactly the same..."

"Well, obviously not every detail will be exactly the same," he growled. "Otherwise it would be the same universe. There are infinite alternatives out there, and in the vast, vast majority the events are so colossally different – Elodie never played that gig or was never born at all, or they never invented the electric guitar, or the Earth never formed – that they're of no practical use. What my bee does is find the ones where the differences are smallest, where the events are closest to ours. That's what I mean when I say probabilistically congruent, you see..."

"Don't patronise me!"

"I'm just explaining –"

"No, don't explain. Shut up."

For once, he did. The car crested a rise and whispered along a cloister of pines. Then another loch appeared, this one smaller, with a shingle beach. A grey heron was stalking the shallows and, at the precise moment that I passed, it speared down and came back up with a brown fish in its beak, an arc of water trailing like pearls. Beautiful and savage, and gone. What were the chances of my seeing that, I wondered? In how few congruent universes had the car, the heron, the fish coincided? I hoped mine was the only one.

"And you," I said, not even sure if Pawel was still on the line. "Being there on the car? How was that possible?"

"I almost did come back up there in person, Fizz."

I flicked him back on. Stared hotly at his face that wasn't his face, that wasn't anyone's face. The number of times that I'd wished he could be with me were uncountable, and right then I'd have given almost anything for him to be sitting in that car beside me so that I could slap that face, whatever it really looked like. "Almost?"

He shrugged. "Almost enough. For your bee to show me there."

"*Almost enough*? Oh, you arrogant fucker." Those last words leaked out of me like puncture air.

"I'm sorry, Fizz. I really would have been there if I could." Then, gently he asked the question I'd been dreading because talking about it meant thinking about it, and that was what I'd been trying to avoid since it happened. "You know who it was that exposed you?"

I shrugged wearily. "Who knows? Some arsehole who picked me at random, who saw your poxy security mods as a challenge and, by the results, not much of one."

His lip curled. "You don't really believe that. People don't get exposed on a whim."

I wanted to go back to the peacefulness of watching the sun on the water, to the heron spearing her lunch uncaring of being observed, but I knew he wouldn't let it lie until he had made his point. "Fine, okay, so it's not random. But it can't be me they want to discredit. It must be Elodie. Even if she is just an old woman with Alzheimer's who no one remembers now."

"Oh plenty of people remember her," he said. "But you're right, there's no advantage to discrediting Elodie now. So it's not her, and it's not you, but maybe someone else close to you…"

"If you mean *yourself*, then just say so," I said coldly. "How is disgracing me going to affect you?"

"The bee," he replied. "It can see *everything*, Fizz. It's the start of the Panopticon."

Secrets have a way of getting out, Pawel told me. *However safe you think they are, whatever security you've put in place. A moment of indiscretion, an easily guessed password, a chink of opportunity, a slice of blind luck. Even the toughest encryption, given enough time, can be broken. Nothing can ever be one hundred percent secure, and if you believe that there are an infinite number of universes where every possible eventuality is played out, that means that somewhere there's at least one where it has.*

Imagine a world where there is no privacy. None. Not for private citizens, not for governments. Not your kid's birthday surprise. Not the cancer diagnosis you don't want to worry your family with yet. Not your affairs. Not your seditions. Not your fiddled expenses. Not your nepotism or your trade agreements or your arms deals or your launch codes. None of it secure. All of it open to scrutiny and display.

That is Panopticon.

And it was all possible because of Pawel's bee. The ability of its quantum mind in this universe to pluck observations from quantum minds in dumb drones in others. Even allowing for the possibility of those tiny discrepancies, like the password for Jean Reynolds' car, it made the idea of keeping a secret from someone who owned such a bee obsolete. And if you had enough of them, the power of vision could belong to everyone.

Can you imagine that? I couldn't. Not then. I hardly understood the words. But that, apparently, was what Pawel had created. And he loved the idea.

"What will happen?" The car had begun to climb the stony

farm road that would deposit me at the bothy where I believed Gordon Templeton had chosen to hide. "Will there be anarchy?"

"Honestly?" Pawel pulled at his lip. "I don't know. Probably. For a while."

"And then?"

"And then it'll be different."

The building at the top of the road was tiny. It had flaking whitewashed walls, a mossy slate roof and windows cataracted with grime. A pile of car tyres stood beside the door; they had slumped and the weeds that proliferated the yard had grown up through the rings. I circled the house, trailing my fingers around the walls, surprised at how cold the stone was, even in the sunshine. Cold, and long abandoned.

The door was locked, so I sat on the step and enjoyed the view down over the wide valley. The green brown scrub of heather, the meandering ribbon of the road that had brought me here. The surprising blue of the last loch. The air was so fresh it chilled my lungs, and the perfume of the nearby gorse thickets made me dizzy. The only sound was the droning of bees, real ones, engaged in their slow tours of the golden blossoms. So unlike the machines we had in the cities, and not even that similar, now that I got a chance to compare them, to Pawel's creation.

In the car, the beautiful machine had helpfully crawled into its container. Now I placed the plastic box on my lap. As if sensing that it might be required, the drone perked up. I just didn't know if I was going to use it or not. Part of me still didn't believe that the bee could do what it did, let alone Pawel's explanation of how. But if I could get the footage, didn't I owe it to Elodie to try?

If I believed Pawel, it didn't matter that Gordon Templeton wasn't here. The number of times the route I'd followed had appeared on his map meant it had been a strong option for him, which also meant that somewhere he had followed it. And the chances were decent that in choosing to come to a place that was all but out of WatchNet's scope, he might have taken a chance on watching that most precious thing that he would never have dared watch at home after all the recent interest in it: mine, Muldoon's and that of whoever else had come calling.

In the end, it was my own curiosity that made me open the box. "Show me Gordon Templeton here," I said.

It wasn't like it had been at his flat. There, even with his sparkwire fetish, the potential that a bee might have snuck in still had to be considerably higher than finding one up here so far from a population centre. So there was no fluster of images, but that didn't mean there would be none at all. The bee hovered at the door of the cottage, sniffing close at first and then swooping out and up to provide a full view of the entrance. To begin with the feed was unchanging. A sequence of nows that were probabilistically identical. Just the door, the walls, the spilled tyres and the few square feet of stony ground around them. Then the subtle differences crept in. It was raining, it was sunny, and then rain again. There was a robin on the step. A hedgehog snuffling among the tyres. Then, miraculously, a car. Barely more than a glimpse of white bumper and a long shadow. It persisted less than a second and over the subsequent long minute when it failed to reappear my hopes all but evaporated.

Then I gasped because not only was the car back, the door was ajar and we were piggybacking the feed of a WatchNet bee as it drifted into the house. The picture was all but black until the camera adjusted to the lighting inside and I could make out the furniture of a kitchen. There were dilapidated olive green formica units on two sides. Missing drawers and cupboard doors with broken handles. A narrow two-ring stove, its oven door and high grill caked with something that made me hope Gordon would never use it to prepare food in any universe. The slabs of canned food and bottled water from his flat were piled beside it. In the middle of the room was a wooden table, two chairs tucked underneath and the surface covered with graffiti: names and tags, phone numbers and childish obscenities. On the table was an ancient device with a slot and a screen, a portable media player.

The visiting bee, obeying its safety protocols, focussed first on the figure stretched out on the horrible couch at the back of the room. Apparently satisfied that Gordon was merely asleep it then turned its attention to the screen of the player and my heart stilled. The definition was poor, but I still saw that this was Elodie. The sound saturated badly with the hubbub of the crowd, but I still recognised her voice.

The venue really hadn't changed that much: I recognised the shape of the stage, the beam that split the low ceiling. I'd even guessed the cameraman's position at the side almost exactly. Elodie was front and centre, a vest top and cut-off denims displaying her years of self-inked protest. Her hair was sweat-slicked, her face flushed, eyes squeezed shut and the muscles of her body, even though the song she strummed was a gentle enough tune, were clenched so tight that it looked like she might drop from exhaustion at any second. I knew, from all of that, and from the shining faces of her fans as Gordon panned away from the stage to show the crush of heads and bodies that filled the venue, that this was the end of the show. The last song. It was a sweet thing about gratitude and the audience knew all the words, for the most part in fact drowning out even Elodie's amplified voice. It wasn't one of her tunes, though. It was a cover and, even as I tried to wrack my brains to remember the title, it was over and she opened her eyes, and smiled and nodded once before unplugging her guitar and leaving the stage. The footage ran on for several minutes after that, though the applause was perhaps not as rapturous as I might have expected. The calls for encores sounded more like pleading.

When the media player went dark I wanted more than anything to be able to reach across universes and wind it back. But if I'd got lucky with the timing of things with my heron this was the opposite, and there was nothing I could do.

It was impossible to refute Pawel's explanations now, outlandish as they were. And the magnitude of my bad luck was only just becoming apparent. The heaped probabilities that his miraculous bee could have located another universe where Gordon Templeton had not only come to this shit hole in the hills, but had chosen to watch the undestroyed gig footage at the precise moment that a random, far-wandering WatchNet bee had come into the bothy and at the same moment in time that I'd happened to be looking for it in this universe… had to be miles from *congruent*. And to have come so close was worse than to have not come at all.

Then the screen winked to brightness again as the video looped back to the beginning. I screamed at my bee to record what it was seeing.

Sitting on the cold doorstep of that awful little house, I watched the performance all the way through. By the time it was over for the second time I thought I understood why Gordon had been so protective. The faces he panned around were mostly young, teenagers or slightly older, glowing with idealism. Even across universes, the love in that room was palpable. The sense of moment and connection. I wondered what it would be like to have something like that, but in my time people were too concerned with the opinions of others to ever be so open in their adoration.

I wondered whether in any of those kids even a scrap of that openness had survived as their world had changed around them, or if, like Gordon Templeton, they had locked it away inside vaults of iron fear or tempered cynicism. Who had this boy become? Had he shorn his dreadlocks and become a bank manager? Or this girl with the khaki vest top and the home-made NOSX tattoos on her freckled arms? Had she scrubbed the tats and gone on to scold her children about web security as she discovered that she suddenly had something to lose? And if the universe where Gordon had come here and watched this was probabilistically so remote from my own, what did such speculations matter? I recognised that I was looking at a version of events as they might have happened. A fiction. But it was all I had.

All of this from one beautiful bee...

But was there just one? In all those universes there must be others, mustn't there? Maybe hundreds, thousands, being used all the time. In worlds where Panopticon had already happened. And, the logic told me, every time we used this bee, we made our universe a tiny bit closer to them. My heart hollowed as I realised what bringing Elodie's gig into existence here may have cost our universe. I convinced myself that only using the bee a handful of times couldn't make a difference. That we were still a long, long way from Panopticon.

With nothing keeping me in the north, I had to finally face up to going home, to the family and friends whose calls I'd blocked and whose messages I'd still not read. The mass disapproval of my peers. The prospect terrified me, but it had to happen. I gave the car instructions and replayed the gig one more time, submerging myself in vicarious camaraderie again. I smiled and cried and sang along with the songs. I imagined myself squeezed in just behind tattoo girl and dreadlock boy, bouncing and shouting with them. On stage, Elodie was sparky and engaging, but the whole thing, from the moment she shuffled barefoot onto stage and shyly plugged in her guitar to the moment she disappeared behind the curtain at the end, was also tinged with an ethereal wistfulness. She didn't talk – not even to explain the circumstances of the show let alone engage in anything that could remotely be described as political agitation – she just sang her songs. Because there was nothing that needed to be said. Everyone in that room knew that they were taking part in some sort of goodbye. A tacit admission of defeat.

I loved the Elodie I saw on that stage, her fire and her dignity and, as the car eased me back down the southward road, I shed a tear knowing that this woman would soon be lost to herself.

And she was right about the song, *Panopticon*. Of course she was. It was the fulcrum of the night, a quiet centre amid all the abandoned protests, a moment of collective held breath. *Panopticon* wasn't a song of anger; it was sweet and simplistic and almost naively wistful.

> *If you could see all of me, every last thing*
> *And I could see you, eagle-eyed, eagle spied from above*
> *If we knew all that's to be known, everything*
> *There'd be no reasons to fight*
> *There'd be no barriers, no barriers to our love*

It was only at the end that it twisted, became embittered:

> *But if it comes, when it comes*
> *Will I like you? Will you like me?*
> *Or will we all be the lonely ones?*
> *The lonely ones. The lonely ones.*
> *When the Panopticon comes.*

Five

The car was no longer moving. A breakdown? I relished the opportunity to hole up in my cocoon for however long it took the rental firm's maintenance team to reach me, but there was no malfunction alert. The car had simply come to a halt. When I tried to get it started again, the vehicle failed to respond. According to the map, I wasn't even on the main road any more.

I cleared the screen and peered out into a darkness that roiled around the car like dense smoke. A gyring pall of bees. When I moved, the closest ones darted towards the window, ticking on the glass like hail.

I was still staring out at them in disbelief when the car door opened and someone slid into the seat beside me. Muldoon had come in uniform this time, buttons gleaming against the black material. She removed her hat and placed it in her lap, smoothed her hair into neat order. A few of the swarming bees from outside had followed her inside. They spun in front of my eyes, and I imagined their traffic load skyrocketing. Muldoon tutted and did something in her face and one by one the bees dropped into the footwell.

"You're something of a celebrity today, Rhian," she said. "You've been trending on *Notorious* since you pulled your little vanishing trick." She smiled without humour. "We'll talk about how you managed that shortly, but for the moment I think the viewing public will be satisfied to see their desperate fugitive at last at the mercy of the law. They just don't need to hear what we're going to say." I opened my mouth, perhaps to protest, I don't know if I was capable of that, but she forestalled my interruption anyway. "Trust me, I'm doing you a favour. Most of them out there wanted a high speed car chase and a gun battle. That's popularity for you."

Then she said: "Play," and Elodie reappeared on my windscreen again. We watched, sharing a weird silence. I disliked having to share them, the singer and the audience, especially since Muldoon appeared entirely unmoved by what she was watching. When she finally spoke, however, I realised that I'd misinterpreted her glassy stare for disinterest. "If anyone were to invent a time machine, this is the one thing I'd use it for. To see her at that show, to be part of it. Even watching this miracle, I can't even imagine what it must have been like to be there when Panopticon started."

I stared at her. "You? You're involved in this nonsense?"

Muldoon slid her gaze towards me and her eyes were shining. "Nonsense? Rhian, we live in an unequal world. And Panopticon is not only our only hope of ever breaking free… it's inevitable."

"I don't understand."

She arched an eyebrow. "It's pretty simple," she said. "We at the project have been working towards the goal of Panopticon for decades."

"We? You mean them?" I indicated the screen.

She snorted scornfully. "That lot? Hardly." The camera panned back to dreads and tats again, their goofy idealism. "No, but they started it, and then we took it on. We are a group of politically likeminded and technologically adept individuals with the will and the skills to make Panopticon happen."

It all clicked into place. "You're talking about… Pawel?"

Muldoon straightened her smart chequered cravat. "We knew him as Matts. He was one of our best and brightest, and there were signs that he might be getting somewhere with distributed quantum entangled networks. Then he went dark on us. We'd let him work unsupervised and trusted him to share his work when the time was right. You might call us naïve, and you'd be right. Anyway, we lost him and we thought he was gone for good."

"Until I started working for Elodie Eagles, and you took an interest in my life…"

"And discovered that your good old fuck-buddy was our man, yes. And now it seems he didn't cut ties with us out of a pang of conscience after all. He's been working away, hasn't he? Such a busy little bee."

"I don't know what you mean…"

"Don't arse me about, Rhian. We know he perfected it, and we know you've been using it. First to pull that clever little switch with the cars. Right up until that moment, you were the easiest tail we've ever had. Next thing we knew we couldn't get a bee in your location. And that's nothing compared to this." She indicated the footage. Elodie's eyes were closed and she was singing with her lips pressed against the grill of the microphone, her words distorted whispers. "You know that most of us didn't believe a recording existed? There's a reason Templeton and his ilk are as paranoid as they are. We tried so many ways to get him to give it up, but he was the stubbornest son of a bitch."

"How can you people get away with this?"

"You think Panopticon is some big secret? Everyone's heard of it, and the authorities want to know so very badly if it really exists that I've a mandate to do anything that I deem necessary, although, of course, I'm not going to tell them anything. I can't tell you how handy it's been to have such liberally sanctioned means. It's just our ends that differ. So, come on. Fess up. What happened?"

I paused, trying to find the words that would allow me to weasel out of it but Muldoon's calm presence brooked no lie. "Fine," I said. "I'm pretty sure Gordon destroyed it. The original, I mean. In our... universe."

Her eyes shone. "But in another one not too far away?"

I nodded. "He simply couldn't and he'd been watching it up in that house. And I recorded it."

"Thank you." Muldoon whispered it. Tears had started to tumble down her cheeks.

"If it's so much of a deal, I'll send you a copy." I felt that I was betraying Elodie, and Gordon, and all of the rest of them, but what choice did I have?

She laughed, a snotty sound. "Save yourself the bother. We already took it."

"Oh."

"Oh, indeed."

"What do you want from me, then?"

"Isn't it obvious? We want the bee. You've got what you wanted from it, Rhian, but that bee was made for us. Hand it over and we'll leave you alone for good."

"Maybe he made it for you," I said, trying not to think of the bee in my jacket pocket. Sure that the outline of the box must be obvious. "But he changed his mind."

"Oh, Rhian." Muldoon shook her head. "Don't even get into playing games with me. I'd have thought you'd have come round to our way of thinking after what happened to you. You have no secrets, girl. You're liberated."

I swivelled then to face her with a righteous anger that snapped my hand up, and it was only the corresponding agitation in the swarm outside that made me turn what would have been a slap to a finger pointed at her face. "That was you?"

Muldoon's smile was so supercilious I regretted not striking her after all. "Actually, no," she said. "Don't get me wrong, it's a tactic we've used before to get our way, but on this occasion someone else got there first."

"Who?" But I saw the answer in her face. "Oh, *piss off*. Why would you even think I'd believe that he would do that?"

Her shrug was slight, as if the issue was inconsequential. "He's been playing you, Rhian. All the way. My guess is he feared our hold over you and reckoned that by removing it he'd free you to continue to do his bidding. Who knows what his motives are? But he's not finished with you yet."

"If that's the case then you can just fuck off. You'll get nothing more from me."

Muldoon's smile cooled into a thin line. "The masses want a car chase, Rhian. It would be the simplest thing to give them what they want, and who knows, maybe on those tight mountain roads something might fail…" I couldn't keep the fear from my face, and she saw it. "Just give me the bee."

I sighed, and nodded. Then indicated the footwell where the three dead drones had fallen. "It's one of those, you idiot." The panic that shadowed her face was fleeting, but it bolstered me.

"Don't lie to me…" She grabbed me by the collar and reached over to pat me down. She found the box immediately and pouted sarcastically as she retrieved it. The lid was open, the box empty.

"What reason do I have to lie?" I'd been lying all my life after all. It was as easy for me as breathing. Now I used all that experience to keep the relief from trembling my voice, to stop myself looking for the bee. "As you've taken such pains to explain, I'm all out of options. It was right here in the cabin observing you when you got in."

Muldoon scooped the devices up from the floor, prodded them with her finger. They rolled, unresponsively in her palm and each of them with their black plastic and yellow stripes and their filmy wings, was identical. "Which is it?"

I shrugged. "He made it look like a regular bee. That's rather the point of infiltration, I gather. I do hope you can fix it."

Carefully, Muldoon slipped the bees into her jacket pocket.

"It was only a mild targeted EMP pulse. I'll find out if you're lying to me soon enough."

I shrugged once more, hoping that Pawel's bee wasn't similarly lying inert under my seat. "One day I'll wake up in a world with no secrets, won't I? And none of this will matter anymore."

"You can absolutely count on that," she said, and got out of the car.

I didn't want to believe that it was Pawel who had exposed me, but Muldoon's explanation of why he might have had a ring of believability. I couldn't think of a single reason why she would lie about it either; except perhaps spite, but I honestly didn't think she cared enough to bother. I spent most of the protracted journey home worrying about what she'd d0 when she discovered my pathetic ruse. I didn't believe that she'd make the car crash, not at least without getting the bee out first, but every jolt in the road felt like the prelude to the cutting of the car's power and a second, less civil, visit. I didn't sleep a wink in the rented capsule in Glasgow either, and by the time I was on the train to Bradford I just wanted to hide from everything. But there was no hiding: not from the rolling nimbus of drones which had dogged me since Muldoon pulled me over, and not from the looks and mutterings of my fellow passengers when they worked out who I was.

I didn't call Pawel. It was less onerous to face the mountain of messages, and once I'd begun I was shocked to find that they weren't nearly as bad as I'd feared. The banks and so forth had instantly locked me out of my accounts for my own security, so all I really had to worry about there was finding a way to prove who I was. Many of the personal communications, from friends and strangers alike, expressed commiseration. And many more were actually interested, asking for interviews, soundbites, tick endorsements. There were even a handful of enquiries for work:

honest, warts and all, memoirs. Not only that, overnight I'd somehow transformed from a pariah into something of an antihero, and I had a sequence of notifications that filled my face with brass band music and the garish blossoms of animated fireworks to congratulate me on breaking my perticks record on the hour, every hour since I'd gone to sleep.

Of course there were horrible messages too. Plenty of them from moralists ladling on the self-righteous scorn, with many going on to speculate on worse crimes that somehow hadn't come to light yet but surely would. And I wasn't short-changed on my share of blind hatred either but, in the context of everything else, I felt I could deal with it.

For perhaps the first time in my adult life, I took succour from my mother's advice: namely that every one of those chastisers did so with their backs pressed to their own bursting closet doors.

The lobby of my apartment building was literally crawling with bees. They clotted the walls like a growth, forming restless patterns and furred clumps from floor to ceiling. When I arrived, they erupted into activity like flies on a carcass. I ran to the elevator, but wasn't fast enough to prevent a skein of them entering too. They alighted on the mirrored walls and peered down at me. One of them landed on my shirt, the weight of it almost imperceptible on my breast as it crawled purposefully across and attempted to squeeze between my shirt buttons.

"*Piss off.*" I flicked the device to the ground and stood on it, relishing the crunch.

I managed to lose most of them at my apartment door, but a few were still too nimble. They followed me to my living room where I dumped my bag, then to my kitchen where I poured a large glass of red wine. I drank it at the table by the window. Pawel's lilies were luminous in a wedge of sunlight. The bees buzzed around them, crawled all over the card.

I gave in and looked to see what the masses were saying. There were hundreds of conversations, with tags ranging from business grievances to revenge sex, from memoir enthusiasts to the worst kinds of *there-but-for-the-grace* gossip. Many of these were now seeing a surge of new activity around the subject of the flowers. *Who were they from? Did Rhian have a lover? Is that who she went to Scotland for? Is she so upset because it all went horribly wrong? Aw, poor Rhian, stupid bitch. Hasn't she killed herself yet?*

There were pictures too, mostly the sex ones, vilely captioned or grotesquely modified. I flicked through them, weirdly calm as if it was all happening to someone else and unable to see how any of it mattered. So they had all my data. What more could they do to harm me? They already knew how little money I had, and many of the threats employed in the old days of doxxing only worked because people could be so much more easily anonymous in those days. Was someone really going to assault me in the street live on WatchNet?

The only thing that really jolted me was the fellow who had made what looked like videos of himself in my flat; standing in the living room, smelling the flowers, watching me sleep. I knew none of it was real, but it was hard not to admire his mixing skill even while I despised him for making me check my log footage to make sure, and for making me wonder about the congruence of realities in which such a thing might actually happen.

I drank the first bottle of wine too quickly, and my struggle to uncork the second caused such hilarity on the streams that had sprung up since my return home that I took bottle and glass through to my bedroom. The bees followed me as far as the threshold, where I was relieved to see that my laughingly obsolete privacy options remained in place. I stared with what I hoped came across as sneering defiance into each one of the tiny cameras hovering before slamming the door. The online outrage was the most satisfying thing I'd felt in ages.

Pawel and I had a secret emergency signal. Three strong buzzes on an intimate piercing, a gap, then another three. Our version of an SOS, a joke thing for when one of us wanted the other in a hurry. We'd only ever used it during the most intense period of our relationship, and that had been months ago. I buzzed him now, then settled down to do some reading and distract myself with the news while I waited.

My face was all over the lead pages, next to that of Angela Hardwick. The bitch was using me as an example – a warning – and the approval ticks for her bill were soaring. I played the report, saw my neighbours complaining that their house prices had plummeted, my landlord saying if they'd known what kind of person I was they'd never have rented me a flat in their lovely development. Then back to Hardwick again, actually slapping fist into palm as she addressed the House. "Secure, controlled sharing of personal data protects us all. The citizens and organizations of our communities deserve to know if someone among them is a risk," she said. "Financially, medically, emotionally. Those with nothing to hide have nothing to fear."

She was a small woman, a little bowed at the shoulders, as if the burdens of her life had been heavy ones. Her hair, which had once been the colour of honey, was mostly grey and cut severely, as was her suit. But it was the shining zeal in her eyes that I recognised.

"Oh, Angela," I said. "What happened to you? How did you become your own enemy?"

Then she was gone and I was back in Hell. A rat princess facing a golden dragon.

"You rang, milady?" The dragon waggled his eyebrows.

"Shut up," my rat replied. "Let me say my piece, okay?"

To his credit he took the warning. "Okay," he said. "Shoot."

My rat stood, hands on her hips, tail swishing and whiskers twitching as I sorted through the thoughts, the questions.

"Okay," I said. "First you need to use your magic to get me on a flight to Paris. I need to see Elodie, but without bringing this whole shit circus with me."

The dragon's snout wrinkled. "That's not going to be easy."

"Whatever. Just do it."

"Okay," he said.

"And I need to be able to send a message directly to someone who might otherwise be quite difficult to access."

That raised a draconic eyebrow, but when I gave him the details he acquiesced. "Anything else?"

"The bee. This Panopticon. It's madness. How could you design something that you knew would destroy the world sooner or later?"

"Or create a better world? The governments have a stranglehold and its only getting tighter."

I snorted. "Well there's no way of predicting what will happen, is there? And you're still quite happy to toss that coin."

"It's not as simple as that, Fizz."

"No? Muldoon says it's set-in-stone. That a device like your bee existing anywhere makes it inevitable. The wikis call it an unstoppable probability cascade; every use, every connection drawing the probabilities closer to unity. That sounds pretty much like fucking inevitable to me."

"Muldoon is an idiot who believes only what she wants to believe. And you know my position on wikis. Like I say, it's not that simple. I've no idea how many connections are required to get us to that stage and neither have you. It could be one, it could be a million. There's every chance that true multiversal Panopticon will never happen in our lifetimes. Maybe even not at all."

"But you want it to. You always have. That's why you built the bee in the first place. And you could have used it a million times by now, or built a million bees. Why didn't you?"

The dragon looked at the rat, but said nothing.

"No, instead, you shunted the responsibility on to me. It was on the cards right from my first contact with Elodie, wasn't it? Because you knew all about her, didn't you, fan boy? Why, Pawel? Am I supposed to be the scapegoat, is that it? Did you expose me too? The woman with all the dodgy secrets and nothing to lose?"

"Fizz..." I scowled at him for interrupting, but I'd run out of steam anyway. "Do you really think I'd do that?"

"I... don't know." It was the truth. A few days ago I would have scoffed at it without a second thought, but now... "I don't even think I know you. I don't know your real name or what your face looks like or where you really live or what you do..."

"You know me better than anyone on this planet," the dragon said.

"I thought I did." I shook my head. "So, really, why the bee? You don't just give something like that to someone to help them out with a tricky job."

It took Pawel so long to answer I thought he'd been disconnected from the instance. Then, quietly: "Because I trust you. Because you're a real person and you live in the real world. And I... I don't. Because... Hell, yes, I could try to bring Panopticon about, but I don't know if it's the right thing to do."

"So what was I supposed to do with it? Use it to step my game up to extorting proper celebrities or actual governments? Or simply dox the whole world out of revenge?"

"You could," he said. "Or you could use it for good. I don't know, to locate missing persons or free political prisoners or end wars."

"Pawel, I don't want to be your pet superhero."

"Okay then, you could destroy it."

I actually laughed then. "And you wouldn't even try to stop me?"

"Maybe I'd respect your decision. I think I would."

"So what? You could just make another one."

"Not like that one. That one is perfection and it was a long time in the making. And besides... There was only ever going to be one. Here, anyway. If it failed then I was prepared to wait to see if it succeeded elsewhere."

"Because in a sufficient number of probabilistically congruent universes... you do make another one, or a million, or I don't destroy it at all, and Panopticon will happen sooner or later anyway?"

"It's likely," he said with maddening calm, "but not inevitable."

I curled up on my bed, hugging into a pillow. In Hell, my rat kicked a rock. It rolled into a lava pool and sank with a sizzle.

Eventually he said: "Fizz, are you all right?"

"No," I breathed, wishing for the detached numbness of earlier. "I'm not all right. It's horrible. Everyone knows everything about me. Every. Single. Thing. I can't stand it."

The dragon nodded. "I can't imagine anything worse happening to me."

"Oh, piss off. Don't make this about you."

"It's about us all. Me, I'm addicted to anonymity, terrified of losing it actually. But I can still imagine how it might be if everyone was the same, if there were no need for secrets. And even after all this time I don't think it's an evil idea."

"Pawel... Just answer me straight. Did you do this to me?"

It was the longest pause yet before he said: "I'm not going to tell you, Fizz. I'd prefer that you trusted me, but you've got the power in your own hands to find out, if you want to."

So that was it. Trust him or use the bee again and risk bringing the end of everything another step closer.

The dragon scratched something in fire on the ashy ground. It was a face login. "Memorise this," he said. "Everything you need to get to Paris is in there."

Elodie was surprised, but ushered me into the apartment all the same. "You should have called ahead, Miss Fitzgerald," she said. "I've not had time to tidy, I'm afraid." To me the place looked every bit the casual mess it had on my last visit. This time, at least, the mynah bird was in its cage. It watched me with its golden eye.

"I'm afraid that wasn't possible," I said. "Unless you would've preferred I bring the attention of the world with me."

Elodie tutted. "Don't be so melodramatic girl," she said. "The world doesn't care about you. You're a minor misfortune that others can point and laugh at. Old news by next week."

Her dismissal stung. "Nevertheless," I replied levelly, "any memoir that I write about you will be dismissed as a pack of lies. So, I won't be completing the work. Obviously, I won't be chasing the remainder of the fee but I'm afraid the deposit is unreturnable. I'm sending you a link to the materials I've assembled so far. You're welcome to pass them on to another memoirist if you like or... whatever." In my face, I okayed the transfer and heard a chime from the back of the room somewhere. I guessed that her face glasses were somewhere amid the clutter in the bookcase. Elodie made no move to retrieve them.

"That packet," I said, "doesn't include the footage of the Glasgow gig..."

She leaned forward, dropping the laconic indifference. "You found it?"

I nodded. "Do you mind if I play it?"

"Now?"

I nodded again and I could see that she wanted to dismiss me, but her need for it was too great. "Very well."

I placed a projector on the Moroccan table. Her crowd appeared on the wall, the excited chat popping with laughter as the camera swung round their faces and then focused on the empty stage. As the lights went down, and young Elodie appeared.

Beside me old Elodie stifled a gasp. *"Mon Dieu."*

I watched her as she watched it. The way her lips curled into a smile as she remembered songs she'd not played since that night. She mouthed along to them, and smiled throughout.

When it was over, when the crowd's elation had ebbed and their solidarity crumbled into confusion over those final lines of *Panopticon*, after young Elodie had padded quietly off the stage, her older counterpart whispered. *"Oui,* that's how it was."

She said it with such certainty, such relief, that I didn't challenge her. If it was close enough for her, it was good enough for me.

"You crushed a few dreams that night," I said.

"Mine included." She shrugged. "But we all needed to grow up and stop believing in the impossible."

"And what if it had been possible?" I searched her face. "What if I told you Panopticon was just around the corner? Would you welcome it?"

Her brow furrowed. "Given that you've now stepped back from writing the memoir, I don't think there's any need to make such conjectures."

"No." I laid a hand on her arm. "Really. Right now. If I were to give you the power to uncover any secret, if I were to give everyone that power, would it be a good thing?"

She laughed. "No, it would be terrible. Panopticon was never about equality, it was a warning against government abuse."

I nodded, flipped an image of Angela Hardwick onto the wall. "Case in point?"

"Oh, that woman?" Elodie tossed her hair. "Yes, precisely that."

I rolled the gig video back, displayed in slow motion the final pan around the audience, the confused, dismayed faces. I paused on a girl with long hair. Young Angela's mouth, open in shock was the spit of older Angela's as she made her defiant declamations in parliament.

"That night," I said. "It fired some of your audience up. Inspired them to find a way to make it happen, to make Panopticon a reality. An ultimate anarchy. But for others," I pointed to the images of Angela Hardwick on the wall, "the disillusionment was absolute."

Elodie touched my arm then, her grip hot and firm. "What are you really asking me?"

"I think you've already answered it," I replied.

I made the call from the table in the Café on the corner of *Quai St Michel*. Anyone watching on the gathering gyre of bees would have seen an exhausted woman, an infamous fugitive, a proven pervert, liar and swindler, brazenly not giving a crap what the world thought of her.

In a private shared space, Angela Hardwick watched the five minute clip I'd selected without comment. It ended with Elodie singing:

> *But if it comes, when it comes*
> *Will we all be the lonely ones?*

Then she said: "This is impossible."

"This is Panopticon."

"No." Her voice was small, lacking all her parliamentary command. "I mean it's wrong. It wasn't like that. She sang *Outta My Garden* before *Panopticon*, not *Friends Like You*. And we all knew each other, but that boy with the dreads... I've never seen him before."

It was what I'd expected, congruent but not quite identical. At least it had been close enough for Elodie. "It'd still do the job, Angela," I said. "If it got into public hands. People would question your motives. They'd start to dig, to see what else you've got to hide."

Who knows if there were bees around Angela Hardwick when she was talking to me? Whether she betrayed any sign of panic, or whether she just calmly nodded and then turned casually away so the liptracers couldn't make out what she said next, her voice heavy with resignation. "If you don't mind, I should very much like to see it all."

Six

There's a café in Seville. It has a garden out back with high walls that in the summer bourgeon with bougenvilia. A groaning mass of blooms, all possible shades of pink. One of the local families comes on a Saturday to spend the afternoon sharing olives and bread and plates of tangy *boquerones*. The whole clan from the bristly granddames down to the giggling twins in their white dresses. This is the place I've been coming to write this up. My own memoir. I edge their familial camaraderie, a pariah in their midst. If they know who I am, they're at least decent about not letting it show. Most likely they don't know. Elodie was right: I was a celebrity for a few weeks and then I was no one again. A no one with nothing to her disgraced name: no career, no ticks, no money... no responsibilities, no ties. No reason not to take a leaf out of Pawel's book and reinvent myself. So, I did.

I tell those who ask that I write minor movies. If they pursue the subject I link to some middle of the road rom coms, the kind written by committee. These would be easy lies to disprove, but to my knowledge no one has bothered.

What I really do for money is dig out nuggets of gossip and

sell them to slag rag channels like *Notorious*. I'm already one of their most valuable contributors, although they know me by an invented name and see a face that looks a little different thanks to one last favour from Pawel. I don't know if I've that to thank for never yet having had a visit from Muldoon, but our paths haven't crossed since Scotland.

The people here are nice enough, on the surface anyway. The family smile when they see me, wave *Ola*. A few times they have asked me to join them and I've enjoyed their hospitality.

Today, however, I have a table to myself. There's a bottle of wine, a dish of olives. Two glasses, two plates.

Robert is Northern European, like me. He is tall, if a little slope-shouldered; he is bald but wears a beard. It is dark and sandy and silver, like lichen-spotted stone. He talks about himself too much, but rarely gives anything away beyond what is readily accessible from his Homespace. I know that he runs a modest architecture firm in Aachen, that his children live in Canada, that he enjoys gaming and remix art. That he has come here for a month to get away from all of that. It's enough. He likes me. We like to make fun of people together.

I have not heard from Pawel in over two years. I don't think I ever will again.

Robert has arrived. "How's it going, Fizz?" he said, before going in search of a menu. I smiled, as I always do when he calls me that.

It's like this: I destroyed the bee.

Or I didn't. I use it every day to winkle out some scandal to boost my selfishly affluent sham lifestyle at the expense of some fool who thinks their privacy is worth a damn to anyone.

Or I still have it, in its box, in my pocket. I haven't used it since the bothy, though I'd be lying if said I'd never been tempted. Especially now, as Robert waves and smiles and I imagine… Oh, I imagine all sorts of things that I will never ask him.

But whatever I tell you, you're just going to have to believe me.

If Muldoon was right and Panopticon is inevitable, it'll come out in the wash at some point. All the true truths, all the lies. Sooner or later.

For now I'm content just to be.

About the Author

Neil Williamson's debut novel, *The Moon King* (NewCon Press), was shortlisted for both the BSFA Award and the British Fantasy Society Holdstock Award for best novel. His short fiction has been nominated for the BSFA and British Fantasy awards and, with Andrew J Wilson, he edited *Nova Scotia: New Scottish Speculative Fiction*, which was nominated for the World Fantasy Award. His latest collection of stories is *Secret Language*, published by NewCon Press (April 2016).

Neil lives in Glasgow, Scotland, and is a member of the Glasgow SF Writers' Circle, whose anniversary anthology, *Thirty Years of Rain*, he co-edited in 2016.

NewCon Press Novellas

Neil Williamson – The Memoirist

Alastair Reynolds – The Iron Tactician
A brand new stand-alone adventure featuring the author's long-running character Merlin. The derelict hulk of an old swallowship found drifting in space draws Merlin into a situation that proves far more complex than he ever anticipated.

Released December 2016

Simon Morden – At the Speed of Light
A tense drama set in the depths of space; the intelligence guiding a human-built ship discovers he may not be alone, forcing him to contend with decisions he was never designed to face.

Released January 2017

Anne Charnock – The Enclave
A new tale set in the same milieu as the author's debut novel *A Calculated Life*". The Enclave: bastion of the free in a corporate, simulant-enhanced world...shortlisted for the 2013 Philip K. Dick Award.

Released February 2017

All cover art by Chris Moore.

NEWCON PRESS

Publishing quality Science Fiction, Fantasy, Dark Fantasy and Horror for ten years and counting.

Winner of the 2010 'Best Publisher' Award from the European Science Fiction Society.

Anthologies, novels, short story collections, novellas, paperbacks, hardbacks, signed limited editions, e-books…
Why not take a look at some of our other titles?

Featured authors include:

Neil Gaiman, Brian Aldiss, Kelley Armstrong, Peter F. Hamilton, Alastair Reynolds, Stephen Baxter, Christopher Priest, Tanith Lee, Joe Abercrombie, Dan Abnett, Nina Allan, Sarah Ash, Neal Asher, Tony Ballantyne, James Barclay, Chris Beckett, Lauren Beukes, Aliette de Bodard, Chaz Brenchley, Keith Brooke, Eric Brown, Pat Cadigan, Jay Caselberg, Ramsey Campbell, Michael Cobley, Genevieve Cogman, Storm Constantine, Hal Duncan, Jaine Fenn, Paul di Filippo, Jonathan Green, Jon Courtenay Grimwood, Frances Hardinge, Gwyneth Jones, M. John Harrison, Amanda Hemingway, Paul Kane, Leigh Kennedy, Nancy Kress, Kim Lakin-Smith, David Langford, Alison Littlewood, James Lovegrove, Una McCormack, Ian McDonald, Sophia McDougall, Gary McMahon, Ken MacLeod, Ian R MacLeod, Gail Z. Martin, Juliet E. McKenna, John Meaney, Simon Morden, Mark Morris, Anne Nicholls, Stan Nicholls, Marie O'Regan, Philip Palmer, Stephen Palmer, Sarah Pinborough, Gareth L. Powell, Robert Reed, Rod Rees, Andy Remic, Mike Resnick, Mercurio D. Rivera, Adam Roberts, Justina Robson, Lynda E. Rucker, Stephanie Saulter, Gaie Sebold, Robert Shearman, Sarah Singleton, Martin Sketchley, Michael Marshall Smith, Kari Sperring, Brian Stapleford, Charles Stross, Tricia Sullivan, E.J. Swift, David Tallerman, Adrian Tchaikovsky, Steve Rasnic Tem, Lavie Tidhar, Lisa Tuttle, Simon Kurt Unsworth, Ian Watson, Freda Warrington, Liz Williams, Neil Williamson, and many more.

Join our mailing list to get advance notice of new titles and special offers:
www.newconpress.co.uk

The Moon King
Neil Williamson

The stunning debut novel from one of Britain's finest writers of genre fiction. Shortlisted for both the BSFA Award for best novel and the Holdstock Award.

All is not well in Glassholm. Amidst rumours of unsettling dreams and strange whispering children, society is disintegrating into unrest and violence. The sea has turned against the city and the island's luck monkeys have gone wild, distributing new fates to all and sundry. Turmoil is coming...

"*The Moon King* is a mysterious, luminous read, full of intriguing characters... Beautifully written and thoughtful. Sure to be one of the best debuts of this or any other year."
— *Jeff Vandermeer*

"The sort of book that creeps into your dreams."
— *Chris Beckett, winner of the 2013 Arthur C Clarke Award*

"*The Moon King* is adult, literary fantasy at its best."
— *Eric Brown, in the Guardian*

"*The Moon King* has you hooked from the start."
— *Edinburgh Book Review*

"An intricately constructed, heartfelt novel that does its author proud."
— *Nina Allan, author of The Race*

Available now in paperback, and e-book
http://www.newconpress.co.uk

Secret Language
Neil Williamson

Secret Language gathers together sixteen stories, four of them written especially for this collection, that demonstrate why Neil is one of genre fiction's finest writers. The BSFA shortlisted story "Arrhythmia" provides just one of the highlights in this exceptional volume.

All four of the new stories are excellent, but one of them in particular, "The Death of Abigail Goudy" may just be the best thing the author has ever written.

"Williamson's territories are the liminal experience and the murky corners of the psyche. He is a virtuoso of the fleeting glimpse, a laureate of loss." – *Interzone*

"Williamson nails style and structure to tell of high school hackers heisting music on the streets to create their own mixes."
– *Speculation (of 'Pearl in the Shell')*

"If Williamson is speaking a secret language, it is one that resonates, surprises and entertains." – *Bristol Book Blog*

"A talented writer who transcends genre, and should be bought, read and cherished." – *Shaun Green, Yet Another Book Review*

Available now from NewCon Press

www.newconpress.co.uk

Immanion Press
Speculative Fiction

Dark in the Day, Ed. by Storm Constantine & Paul Houghton

Weirdness lurks beyond the margins of the mundane, emerging to dismantle our assumptions of reality. Dark in the Day is an anthology of weird fiction, penned by established writers and also those new to the genre – the latter being authors who are, or were, students of Creative Writing at Staffordshire University, where editor Storm Constantine occasionally delivers guest lectures. Her co-editor, Paul Houghton, is the senior lecturer in Creative Writing at the university.
Contributors include: Martina Bellovičová, J. E. Bryant, Glynis Charlton, Storm Constantine, Louise Coquio, Elizabeth Counihan, Krishan Coupland, Elizabeth Davidson, Siân Davies, Paul Finch, Rosie Garland, Rhys Hughes, Kerry Fender, Andrew Hook, Paul Houghton, Tanith Lee, Tim Pratt, Nicholas Royle, Michael Marshall Smith, Paula Wakefield, Ian Whates and Liz Williams.
ISBN: 978-1-907737-74-9 £11.99, $18.99

Blood, the Phoenix and a Rose by Storm Constantine

Wraeththu, a race of androgynous beings, have arisen from the ashes of human civilisation. Like the mythical rebis, the divine hermaphrodite, they represent the pinnacle of human evolution. But Wraeththu – or hara – were forged in the crucible of destruction and emerged from a new Dark Age. They have yet to realise their full potential and come to terms with the most blighted aspects of their past. Blood, the Phoenix and a Rose begins with an enigma: Gavensel, a har who appears unearthly and has a shrouded history. He has been hidden away in the house of Sallow Gandaloi by Melisander, an alchemist, but is this seclusion to protect Gavensel from the world or the world from him? As his story unfolds, the shadow of the dark fortress Fulminir falls over him, and memories of his past slowly return. The only way to find the truth is to go back through the layers of time, to when the blood was fresh. ISBN: 978-1-907737-75-6 £11.99, $18.99

Lightning Source UK Ltd.
Milton Keynes UK
UKOW03f0652100217

294041UK00002B/19/P